Chaos in the Pews
CHAMPAGNE'S WRATH

YOLANDA SOTO

SAY IT LOUD PUBLISHING

DELAWARE

Book cover design by Adrijus Guscia
Book interior design by Jodi McPhee
Edited by Sharon Honeycutt

Author's photo by Terrance S. Neal, Sr.
of Bring The Noise Photography
Makeup by Ariel Green

ISBN: 979-8-218-18694-4

Say It Loud Publishing

Printed in the United States of America

*I love and respect my
superhero mom, Barbara M. Soto,
so much that I dedicate this book to her!*

PROLOGUE

Devil's Playground

WHILE DEXTER PLAYS HIS GAME console upstairs, Champagne and her daughters, Corrin and Jazmine, are getting ready for dinner and changing downstairs. After confronting Peaches at the church and learning that Sahara is his daughter, Zion takes a drive to relax. His mind is racing, and he needs some time to himself.

Champagne's throwing pots and pans on the stove and slamming plates onto the dinner table, an unusual display of anger that visibly disturbs Corrin and Jazmine.

Corrin gestures for Jazmine to finish setting the table and says, "We'll help you, Mom." She pauses and inquires, "Why are you so angry?"

Champagne pauses before facing her daughters. "Look at me, girls, and pay attention." The Spencer girls follow their mother's instructions, and they pay close attention to her. "There are people in this world who are envious of our family. They are determined to destroy us because they want what we have. I have always worked hard for this family. I've been able to identify these wolves in sheep's clothing that your father could never. The ungodly union of your father and this whore resulted in the birth of a child. That demon is not your sister! You and your brother are Zion Spencer's covenant heirs. He might introduce you to this bastard, but she'll be just like her mother: a lying little bitch. Because of his weakness, your father fell for Satan's tricks. He turned on me. Never forget what I've told you because I love him and therefore forgive him. Are you following me?" Champagne queries.

The girls all say in unison, "Yes, ma'am."

"Would you like to assist me in completing dinner?"

The girls say it again, "Yes, ma'am."

Champagne and the kids are setting the food on the table when Zion walks in...

"Hello, Dad!" The girls run and embrace their father with joy, reviving his exhausted body with their love. He takes his time to pay each of his daughter's particular attention. Dexter remains upstairs and is not aware that his father has returned home. Zion moves toward the stairs.

"When will we talk about what happened at the church?" chants Champagne.

Zion groans loudly. He sounds exhausted and says, "I'm not in the mood for this right now."

"You cannot leave me now, not even for a moment! I've put up with your deceit, infidelity, and relationships with other women, but a damn child born during our marriage? Zion, what the hell?!" calls Champagne.

"Champagne, please stop pushing so hard! What information do you seek? Yes, ever since we got married, I've slept with Peaches quite a few times. Undoubtedly, her daughter could be my own. I already love that child, yes. I have always loved Dominique, yes. You have known that since before our marriage, but you trapped me. I still can't recall our first night sleeping together. Plans Peaches and I had made for our futures since we were young changed the day I met you. I ought to have refused to give in to your father's demands that I wed you. Are you leaving me then? Are you seeking a divorce?"

Champagne freezes in place, her mouth hanging open and her words appearing to have disappeared.

"Hello?" Zion says, trying to jolt his wife out of her reverie.

Champagne makes no comment. She appears unable to speak or move.

Zion says, "We have discussed the matter at length, and at this point I must head upstairs. It won't be long before I head back down for dinner. Once a DNA test verifies what you and I already know to be true—that Sahara is in fact my daughter—Champagne, I will break the news to the children."

Corrin and Jazmine can overhear a fight between their parents while they are in the dining room. "Yes, Corrin, mother is correct. Daddy can't see."

"Jazzy, let's pray for Daddy because he's in a difficult situation at the moment. This woman and her satanic daughter have a demonic grip on him, and he is powerless to break free. When was the last time you heard our father speak to mother in such a harsh manner?"

"Never," Jazmine says in response.

"I agree; that is absolutely correct," states Corrin.

Dinner is a peaceful time for the family.

≈

A few days later, Zion goes back to work, but he finds he cannot concentrate on the tasks at hand. He researches the United Church of Pentecost and Deliverance's website to find out when and where the next service would be held so he could go. He pays Peaches an unexpected visit in order to get the information he requires from her.

Champagne is on her way to a ministers' gathering when she spots Zion's Tesla parked at United Church of Pentecost and Deliverance. Champagne is interested in this discovery. "He's going to see that whore at that church brothel!" Champagne mutters to herself as she maneuvers her vehicle into a parking spot reserved for a minister at the local church. "I'll park here," she says.

After one hour, the babysitter for the Spencer family gets a phone call from Mother Spencer. She tells the babysitter not to let the children watch the local news.

~

At the ornate Gothic church, Champagne's mother attempts to console her granddaughters, Corinthian and Jazmine. She whispers to them as she holds them tightly in her arms and says, "I pleaded with your mother to divorce your father on multiple occasions. If only she'd listened to me, she could have still been with us, but she had so much love for your father. She couldn't live without him. Her love for him was the final straw that caused her to break. My sweet daughter went insane because of his cruel betrayals, but he stood by and protected his lover and the baby they had together. Because of what he influenced my daughter to do, I will never forgive him. Champagne was a loving mother, a devoted wife, and a woman of God to all of us, but those last hours do not represent who she was. Never let that slip your mind. Both you and your brother were the recipients of an immense amount of love from your mother. Her family was the driving force behind everything she did."

The girls grieve for losing their cherished mother while burying their heads in their grandmother's chest and sobbing their hearts out.

≈

As Zion looks around the sanctuary, he realizes the effect that Champagne's passing has had on the lives of so many people. His focus shifted to look at both of his daughters and Dexter seated next to Mother Spencer. All of it hits him at once: the suffering of his children, Champagne's passing, losing Peaches, the years he did not get to spend with Sahara because of his actions, and the consequences of those actions. Zion's brokenness overwhelms him. While trying to console him, Mother Spencer can't stop her son from crying uncontrollably. Onlookers from a variety of ministries have noticed Zion's inappropriate behavior thanks to Champagne's one-sided diarrhea of the mouth. As a result, they are currently rolling their eyes and discussing him amongst themselves while the funeral is taking place.

"He has the audacity to cry in front of everyone."

"He drove her completely insane."

"We're only a broken heartbeat away from the grave or jail," said a man.

"The more he cries, the less he'll piss."

As she takes one last look at her daughter's lifeless body, Champagne's mother completely loses it. She dashes towards Zion while screaming, "You took away my child! You son of a bitch who cheated, your ass ought to be buried in that coffin!"

"People who are crazy and unstable tend to have parents who are the same. We are all in mourning over the loss of Champagne." While Champagne's mother continues to cause a disturbance, Mother Spencer gives her response. Mother Spencer and Zion gather the children who are crying and then leave the church after reaching the conclusion that it would be best to skip the repast.

They are all completely drained emotionally. After Zion brings his kids inside, everyone takes showers and they change into more comfortable clothes while Mother Spencer prepares a simple meal. Zion continues the pattern that Champagne has established, and they eat dinner in the dining room.

Zion addresses the group while they are picking at their food and says, "We are all going to miss your mother. No one else was quite like her. She loved us with every ounce of her being, and she loved every one of you in particular. No one will ever be able to fill the role that she played in your lives, but in order to get back to some semblance of normalcy, we will need some help.

"Mother Spencer has given us her word that she will move here and continue to be of help to us for as long as we require her. Since you're still in your early teens, I'm going to be straight with you about something. I had a lot of affection for your mother, but at the age we got married—we were still kids ourselves—it just wasn't the right decision. When I was younger, I made some poor decisions, just like everyone else does at that age. If your mother were here, I would like to apologize because I was not the best husband that I could have been to her. I mistakenly believed that in order to be a good husband and father, I needed to provide you with material things rather than my time. I want to start by apologizing for not being the father you needed me to be at the times in your lives when you needed me to be. When you go back to school, there is a possibility that you will hear things about our family that are neither kind nor accurate."

"Are you referring to the daughter that you and the new preacher's wife had together as your bastard daughter? Everything that I needed to know, I learned from the rumors. You watched out for her rather than my mother. I hate you! You are all responsible for the death of my mom!" Corinthian cries out. After shoving her chair back, she dashes upstairs.

It has rendered Zion speechless because of the outburst made by his daughter.

The Spencer family matriarch chases after her up the stairs.

"Is that what the two of you think?" Zion addresses his inquiry to Jazmine and Dexter.

"It was told to me you routinely cheated on our mother with a variety of other women. Is that what you mean?" asks Dexter.

"Yes. I cheated on my partner, but it was only with one other woman and not multiple ones."

Jazmine asks, "Do you have a daughter with another woman?"

"Yes. Sahara is the name of your younger sister. You're all brilliant, beautiful Spencer children. I know that this is going to be a challenging transition for all of us, but I want you to know that my blood connects to all of yours. I'm hoping that you'll be willing to extend a warm welcome to your younger sister as a member of our family. I will do whatever it takes to bring our family closer together. My relationships with each of my children are the gifts that I value the most. I was in the wrong, and I will do whatever it takes to mend the relationships I have with each of you. Are you able to forgive me?"

"Yes!" exclaims Dexter.

"We love you, Daddy!" chimes in Jazmine.

Zion holds on to his children with all of his might. "I love you, too. I am truly sorry for the suffering that I have brought upon you We are going to make it through this."

≈

When Mother Spencer knocks on the door to Corinthian's bedroom and opens it, she discovers her granddaughter sobbing across the bed with her face buried in her pillow.

Corinthian screams, "Get out of here!"

"You are well aware, Corrin, that Mom-Mom loves you beyond the stars and beyond the moon. This is a difficult and emotionally taxing time for all of us. For showing disrespect for your father, however, I will not give you a pass. If your mother had heard how you spoke to your father, she definitely would have had a fit. After we have finished talking, you will head downstairs to confront him with your apology. Do you understand me?"

Corrin responds, "Yes, ma'am," while concealing her face further in her pillow.

"Rise to your feet and explain to me where you heard that poison you were spewing downstairs."

"People from the church mentioned it to me and by members of my family. Is it true?" inquires Corrin.

"That a good lie will almost always contain some element of truth is one of the worst things about it. To answer your question, yes, your dad is Sahara Rothschild-Patterson's biological father, and Dominique Rothschild-Patterson is her mother. Zion would do nothing to cause physical harm to another person, and especially not to your mother. Your father and Dominique were childhood friends. Before he met your mother, they were high school sweethearts. However, adultery is adultery, regardless of whether it involves my son. He's erred and admitted his guilt. He is sorry for his behavior and asks for your forgiveness. I can't tell you how you should feel about this circumstance, but Sahara is innocent. She does not have any say in the matter of who her parents are or any influence concerning their decisions. What I want to bring to your attention is the love and compassion that Christ has for us, despite our sins. He is the ultimate judge in all matters."

She took a pause. Mother Spencer poses the question: "Do you have any other questions for me?"

"No, ma'am. In just a few minutes, I'll be heading back downstairs to finish dinner. I have to use the restroom. Please excuse me."

"Okay, baby. I love you."

"I love you, too, Mom-Mom."

Corrin walks into the Jack-and-Jill style bathroom that she and Jazmine share as Mother Spencer exits the bedroom and rejoins the rest of her family downstairs. She splashes her face with the icy water, then dries it off with a hand towel while staring into the mirror. Then she turns off the freezing water.

"Momma, you were my best friend. I miss you so much. I know Daddy hurt you. When I heard you crying in your room by yourself at night, I used to pray for you. I'll apologize and forgive him as you would, but that woman and her daughter killed you. They forced you to leave me too soon, and I despise them both. I'll never accept her! I'll play nice to keep the peace, but I'll never betray you by accepting that bastard as my sister. Jazmine is the only sister I have and the only sister I require in my life. I'll honor you and your memory by being the example you set for others. I hope I make you proud. Momma, I love you." Corrin then heads downstairs to be with her family.

Corrin finds herself entangled in the web of deceit that her mother wove, and she makes a solemn oath to exact vengeance by inviting Champagne's wrath into her life.

Over time, the Spencer Clan has grown up and become well-liked members of the community. Corinthian is elevating her mother's standards by being a captain on the cheerleading squad, an honor student currently enrolled in college courses while still a senior at her elite private high school, and a huge fashionista! Jazz can practice her creative nail art and out-of-the-box hairstyles with the help of her friends. She is an outstanding student and works wonders with her hands. Young Dexter is a dashing and bright young man who, just like his father, is showing an aptitude for the world of business.

Zion has done an excellent job of raising his children with the help of Mother Spencer, his extended family, and Champagne's parents. He wishes Champagne could see how much their kids have grown and developed. Thoughts of Sahara, his youngest daughter, who experienced so much tragedy at such a young age, interrupt Zion's contented reflection. When she found out Zion was her father instead of her uncle, Sahara was bewildered but ultimately relieved. Tragically, she now has PTSD and nightmares after the shooting.

Through therapy and positive reinforcement, her parents and Zion attempt to help her. In contrast, Sahara's visits every other week are met with teasing from Corrin and Jazz who chant, "Home-wrecking bastard and killer of mothers!" Sahara is the target of constant verbal abuse from Champagne's daughters who mock her because of her darker skin. Her half-sisters take great pleasure in making Sahara feel unwanted and unworthy, but Dexter is always there to defend her. Contrary to his sisters, he does not dislike her. He cherishes his family, especially his father's face, as it brightens whenever Sahara is around.

Sahara doesn't tell her parents about the horrible treatment she gets from her sisters because she blames herself for their mother's death. She takes the abuse as a sacrificial lamb for many years until a twenty-year-old church musician notices the stunning teen at age fifteen. After Zeke Channing convinces Sahara to keep their relationship a secret for months, she falls deeply in love with him. During this time, Sahara feels empowered and unstoppable because she and Zeke are together against the world. But when Sahara gets pregnant, he leaves the state without saying why and without giving her a new address. As Zion fills in as a surrogate father, he and her parents feel like they've failed her again. Corrin and Jazz accuse her of following in her mother's footsteps by becoming a whore. Sahara maintains a positive outlook and sticks with it until she passes the GED exam.

Sahara, who doesn't want sympathy or a handout, is determined to make her own way without the financial help of her wealthy parents. Sahara is a mother who is stubborn and works hard. She wants to give her daughter a good life and sees problems as opportunities. Her parents admire her tenacity but caution her not to be too proud to accept help if she requires it.

CHAPTER ONE

Next Lifetime

I T WAS A SWELTERING DAY in the middle of summer and all the children in the neighborhood were outside having fun playing tag, hopscotch, freeze tag, and kickball. Meanwhile, a group of preteen girls rhymed while playing double Dutch. Their classmates and friends surrounded the young women as their neighbors looked on from their open windows and front porches. Their acrobatic prowess was remarkable as they kept up with the escalating rate at which the ropes were turning. Teenage boys who had just finished playing basketball looked exhausted and sweaty as they eagerly joined the excited crowd to find out what the commotion was about.

One of those boys, Zion Spencer, makes his way out of the crowd to watch as his girlfriend, Dominique Rothschild, performs a standing split while keeping pace with her friends who are quickly turning the ropes while the crowd yells, "Faster!" Zion watches mesmerized as Dominique stealthily glances at him but still maintains eye contact with him. She then performs a backflip to free herself from the ropes without contacting them, and another jumper takes her place. As go-go music continues to play in the background, we can hear the crowd screaming, yelling, and making beats on anything that is close to them. As Dominique makes her way toward Zion, she smiles and waves to the people gathered there.

"You're going to have a brother fighting with moves like that, girl."

"There's no need for violence. I only have eyes for you. Everyone is aware of this."

Zion kisses Dominique on the lips tenderly. "Girl, I adore you."

"I love you even more." Zion moves in for a hug, but she stops him. "I'm perspiring."

"Me, too, but I still want to hold you."

Dominique relents, and they walk home together, holding hands.

He asks, before she rushes up the stairs, "Do you want to watch a movie later? Set It Off, starring Queen Latifah, or The Long Kiss Goodnight, starring Samuel L. Jackson?"

"I need to finish my term paper, but if you arrive by seven-thirty, I'll be ready."

"Your mom's on the phone, Peaches," her grandmother yells through the screen door.

"All right. I'll be there."

"How come your family calls you Peaches?"

"My grandma said it's because I was a round, sweet baby. Be here on time!"

"Okay. I will. See you later."

Zion is thinking about the future he and Dominique will create as he walks home. He has a deep, abiding affection for her and knows that feeling will only grow stronger as time passes. Zion rushes up to his room to find the best outfit for his upcoming date. He thinks about all the aftershaves he could use and remembers that Dominique likes the smell of Cool Water the most. Zion gets ready for his date and makes sure he has everything he needs. He finishes getting ready and then checks himself out in the mirror before heading out to meet Peaches. This evening, he will take his mother's car out for a spin.

She says, "I worked a double shift at the hospital, and I'm exhausted. Please get back by midnight."

Zion responds "Yes, ma'am" as his mother hands him the keys to the family vehicle.

Zion runs to the car, his excitement level skyrocketing at the prospect of seeing Dominique once again. After he has arrived at her residence, he takes a moment to clear his throat before knocking on the door.

"Who is it?"

"Zion, ma'am."

Her grandmother walks up and pulls open the door.

"Hello, Ms. Rose. I hope all is well with you this evening."

"I am doing just fine. Baby, please come on in. How is Ms. Gayle doing these days?"

"She's healthy, despite the long hours she puts in at her job."

"Work is something that all responsible single parents do in order to provide for their children, and most of them put a lot of effort into their jobs. Dominique tells me you applied to Morehouse. That is a very impressive educational establishment."

"Yes, ma'am. If I am accepted, it will be a dream come true."

"I will say a prayer for you, but I'm sure that no matter where you end up, you'll make your mother proud," Ms. Rose said.

"Thank you. I'll give it my best shot."

"The only thing you can do is try, and you should never give up."

"Grandma, are you down here putting Zion to death with your ramblings?"

"Leave us alone," her grandmother says. "We're having a good old chit-chat. Isn't that correct?"

As Dominique descends the stairs, Zion watches her from a standing position. Her yellow, sleeveless, gold-belted dress brings out the best in her naturally curly, shoulder-length hair. "Beautiful," he gushes to her. "You are stunning in every way."

Ms. Rose smiles as she notices Zion's love for her granddaughter in his eyes.

Dominique blushes and responds softly, "Thank you," as she retrieves a large purse from the bottom of the stairs. Before leaving for the movies, the two say their goodbyes and hug Grandma Rose.

"What? Your mother let you borrow her car tonight?"

"Yes! I am pumped." Zion opens the car door for Dominique, making sure she's comfortable before closing it.

Dominique asks, "Would you mind if we changed plans and went to the beach instead?"

"Absolutely not, but it is getting dark."

"I'm ready for it."

Peaches takes a full-size blanket and sheet from her bag, along with a pillow, candles, and a lighter, and Zion finds a very secluded section of the beach. She instructs Zion to light the candles, and once he does, they sit on the blanket, facing each other.

"Why are we here, Peaches?"

She reaches out and clasps her hands in his. "This is our final year of high school. You will be attending Morehouse, and I will be attending Howard University. I want to make the most of each and every remaining moment we have together."

"We're going to college, babe. I'm not going to die. We'll have the wedding of your dreams once we graduate. Mrs. Zion Spencer; you will be my wife."

"Mrs. Spencer. I like the sound of that. We'll have five children, a dog, a large house, a large pool for our kids, and a yard large enough for family barbecues."

"What? What about two children and a nice fish tank?" Both of them burst out laughing.

They lie across the blanket, Dominique nestling her head on Zion's chest, gazing at the stars. "I could live in this moment for the rest of my life."

"We will experience a lifetime of similar moments. I am aware that we are still young, but I know what I want, and that is to grow old with you. Regardless of how far our education takes us, you will remain in my heart and soul forever. You make me a more accomplished version of myself. You challenge and inspire me. Dominique, would you marry me?"

"Always and forever, yes."

Zion takes a velvet box from his pocket, opens it, and reveals a stunning, three-stone diamond ring. "It's not quite what you deserve, but it's a sign of things to come." He slips the ring on her finger, and they share their first passionate kiss. "Are you sure we're ready for this?" Zion asks, breaking free.

"I'm going to be your wife, complete with two children and a fish tank. Yes, I'm certain, and I'm prepared."

Dominique screams in agonizing pleasure as she becomes one with Zion, whose skin is electrified by her every touch. This erogenous rage he experiences is unquenchable; the more he takes, the more he wants. The couple can't seem to move on from this moment because they are so engrossed in one another.

When they're done, they lie on the sand with their bodies still entangled, talking about how much they love each other forever. Zion wrapped Peaches in a blanket and gently kissed her on the neck and lips before covering them with the sheet. The moonlight catches the diamonds in her ring as she lays her head on his chest.

Dominique looks down at her hand. "Will we always feel this way, Zion? This is too good to be true."

"This is only the beginning, my beautiful, smart, quirky, one-in-a-million lover and friend. I guarantee it." Zion kisses Peaches passionately, and her body yields to his will as they make love again under a starlit sky.

≈

As Zion reminisces about the life he shared with Peaches and promised to give her, the reality of the life he didn't intend to live causes a flood of tears to fall onto the contracts he was supposed to be reviewing, until the chime of his doorbell frees his mind from the memories. Zion quickly rises from his mahogany-brown leather, tufted chair, wipes his eyes, and walks to his front door, wondering who it could be. A smile spreads across his face as he opens the front door.

"I came to check on you, Daddy," Sahara says, leaping into his arms.

Zion clutches her tightly. "You do not know how much I needed this." He takes a step back and looks at her. "You are stunning. I'm not sure what I did to deserve a daughter like you."

It drew his attention to the sun reflecting off a charm on her necklace. Sahara observes her father looking at it. "Mom stated you gave her this ring when you were younger. She thought I should have it to remember you by."

"That's a very special ring," he says as they walk inside together.

Sahara settles in and starts brewing a cup of coffee. She walks over to her purse and pulls out a circle tin.

"Are those Momma's cookies?" he inquires, smiling.

"They most emphatically are. She insisted I bring them when I mentioned I'd be by to see you. I'm not sure what she does to make them so delicious."

"Momma always said it was the love she put into everything she made."

"I've heard her say that over the years, but I'm convinced she's hiding something else." Sahara pauses before asking, "How are you doing, Daddy? Really?"

"What exactly do you mean, sunshine?"

"I'm worried about you. You're an attractive, successful man. Dating or meeting new people might be a good idea. You live alone in this large house. I care about you and want you to be happy."

"I am content because my children are happy. The business is thriving. What else could a man want?"

"Your own life and someone to share it with."

"The life I have is the life I deserve, and I'm content with it."

"Giving up on joy, love, and happiness, Daddy, will change nothing in the past. It is not your responsibility to atone for Champagne's wrath. It's been nearly two decades. You can't keep holding yourself hostage because of past decisions. You must forgive yourself and move on with your life. This should not be your prison. I miss seeing the twinkle in your eyes. Your eyes are sad when you smile. You keep everything inside and act as if everything is fine when it isn't. In order to move forward, you must address your past emotions. You work from sunrise to sunset. Daddy, that's not living. Have you considered seeing a therapist?"

"You definitely have your mother's candor. No, I've never considered seeking counseling."

"You've spent so much of your life taking care of us; I want to make sure you're taking care of yourself. I don't think you're okay, and more than anything, I want you to experience being in love again. Life is what you make it, you told me when things got tough."

"So," Zion said with a small smile, "you're feeding me my advice?"

"Yes, sir."

"Your mother knew me as well as you do. How is she doing?"

"She's fantastic. She and dad have gone to Africa. They plan to stay for a few months. He is starting a church, and she is setting up a computer lab for kids."

"Is she happy?"

"She's happy and thriving, which is exactly what I want for you."

"All I ever wanted was her happiness," Zion says, "and if she's happy, I'm happy."

"Dad, will you consider my suggestion to get some therapy?"

"Sure, I'll give it some thought. What about my grandchildren?" intentionally changing the subject, Zion asks.

"They're fantastic. I'll have to bring them over to see you."

"Yes, please; I'd really enjoy the company."

"So I'm going to leave now. Is there anything else I can do for you before I leave? I can whip up something quick."

"No, but thank you for caring and checking on your old man."

"Without a doubt. The two of us are inseparable."

He hugs her and tells her, "I love you, pumpkin. She embraces him and gives him a tight hug.

"Call me if you need anything, Dad. I'm not kidding!"

"Okay, I will. Be careful."

Sahara sees herself out, and Zion relaxes back in his chair as she walks out the door. He smiles and shakes his head, remembering his and Dominique's discussion about their future children.

Zion mutters aloud, "One child and fish," as he examines the enormous fish tank in his office.

CHAPTER TWO

It's All About Corinthian

I T'S BEEN ABOUT TWENTY YEARS, and Zion and Champagne's daughter, Corinthian Spencer, has grown into a stunning, intelligent, and successful young woman. As befits a person whose given name is taken from a book of the Bible, no one dares to dispute what she says. Because her mother is biracial, she has fair skin. She has light-brown eyes that go well with her waist-length, wavy chestnut hair. Corrin inherited her father's ambition and zest for life, but beneath her beautiful exterior and selfless acts of kindness, she hides a spirit of hatred and wickedness.

She is even more powerful in the church than her mother was in the whole tri-state area. Corrin has constructed a seemingly delightful image for herself, but her true nature lurks just beyond the light. She behaves as if she doesn't care what other people think, but in truth the approval of others is her main motivator. At all times, she maintains impeccable standards and never overlooks a single detail. Corrin, the daughter of Champagne, only wears the best: she has perfect hair, nails, makeup, and designer clothes. People look to Corrin for advice on how to organize the youth and young adult programs because they assume she has it all together.

Despite her talent and dedication, she drives herself crazy, trying to meet the standards set by her late mother. Corrin spends about six-and-a-half months out of the year on the road giving speeches, seminars, and consultations. The hard work of this strategic opportunist has paid off handsomely. Her multimillion-dollar brand has attracted many influential religious and secular leaders, as well as devoted fans. To young people considering a career in ministry, Corrin is a walking advertisement for holiness as a way of life, not just an ideal to be attained.

Perfectionism is a heavy load, but Corrin wears it like a badge of honor. At the end of her speech to a crowd of five thousand college students in Philadelphia, she exclaimed, "We recognize our fallibility and strive to improve. We want to be the best we can be. Feel good about yourself, have faith in your abilities, keep going even when things look bleak, and don't forget to enjoy yourself as you push through obstacles to achieve your goals. Quit procrastinating and make a difference now. Get it done right now! God bless you and good night." The audience rises to its feet, and Corrin takes a bow to deafening cheers.

Many audience members applaud Corrin as she returns to her dressing room. She really misses her mother and wishes she were here. Corrin rubs Champagne's wedding ring between her fingers as she hears a knock at the door. The ring hangs from a chain around her neck like a charm. "Who is it?" Corrin enquires.

"One of your mom's longtime pals."

Corrin quickly walks over to the entrance and pushes it open. She hasn't had a serious conversation with anyone who knew her mother in years. Corrin has the unmistakable impression that her mother, even in death, can sense when she needs her.

"Please, come in. What's your name?" asks Corrin.

"My name is Zena Whitcomb, and you look exactly the same as when I last saw you a very long time ago. You were nearly an infant. However, Champagne adored all of her children. She did not lead her own life. Champagne believed it was God's will for her to be your mother; she did not take this responsibility lightly. Many of us had professional aspirations when we were in school, but Champagne only ever wanted to be a wife and mother. You comprehend the extent of Champagne's affection for you and your siblings, right?"

"Yes, and daily I miss her. I'm delighted to see you here. Although I don't recall you or my mother mentioning you. I was just thinking about her," Corrin states.

"Nothing about this surprises me. I fell in love, got married, and moved to Paris after high school. I lived there until the passing of my husband from cancer three years ago. I've been back in the United States for nearly a year.

"Champagne and I kept in contact through mail and email. Occasionally we would speak over the telephone, but our conversations were always about her beautiful and intelligent children. It shocked me to learn of her death and the circumstances of it," replies Zena.

A sigh escapes Corrin's lips, and she rolls her eyes.

"I'm sorry to have to say something about that. The foot-in-mouth disease is a real problem for me." It's a playful remark from Zena.

Corrin responds with a strained smile, "I'm used to it, but that doesn't make it any easier."

To which she replied, "Well, it must be cool having another sister."

"Really, it's not! She's a total bust. And my heart goes out to her poor kids. They should have a better mother. Although we share a father, we are not sisters!" Corrin says, clearly repulsed.

Zena questioned, "How are your siblings?" as she tried to switch gears.

"Jazz is fantastic! Her third full-service salon has opened. Dexter is an adult child. Six months ago, he opened his second laser tag and arcade business. My mother would be proud of the legacy she has left. We all miss her every day, but we know she's at peace in the arms of the Master. That brings us comfort," Corrin explains.

"I'm sure your mother is beaming from above. How is your father doing? I haven't seen him in a long time," Zena explains.

"I guess he's fine. We're not even close. We communicate via text or email. I mostly see him on holidays. He never remarried, so I know Momma was his true love. A few women tried, but none could match Momma's devotion to Daddy." Corrin takes a breath before continuing. "I believe Daddy blamed himself for Momma's death deep down in my heart. He was never the same after that. He did his best, raising us with Grandma Spencer's help, but he never seemed to regain that spark in his eyes. He missed none of our school events and came home from work every evening to kiss us goodnight, but it was his passion and vibrancy that made him the great Zion Spencer.

"My heart goes out to my father. He hasn't lived a full life. Dad works himself to sleep most nights, although the company is a financial services behemoth. My father could retire and travel around the world. I'd welcome a deserving woman who could make my father happy once more. He's lost his joy, and I'm at a loss for how to help him. I try not to see him because it breaks my heart. My mother would still be alive and my parents would still be together if it weren't for Dominique and her bastard daughter, Sahara," Corrin says coldly.

Zena, overcome with grief for Zion, sheds a few tears. "I'm at a loss for words. The Zion I remember was full of life and eager to take on tough challenges. Working your life away is a terrible way to live. Oh, Zion!" Zena says quietly.

"I've got an idea! Would you like to meet my father for dinner?" Corrin enthusiastically inquires. "I'm sure you'd have a lot in common, and you're a lovely lady. I know you and my mother had a good relationship. What do you think?"

"I was more of your mother's friend," Zena says. "Zion and I had only met a few times. He's unlikely to remember me."

"That's even more reason to get together for dinner. You two can get to know each other again. Please?" Corrin begs to differ.

"Okay."

"Great! Here's my business card. Please contact me once you've settled in, and thank you very much. I owe you a lot." Corrin kisses Zena goodbye and the ladies say their farewells.

Zena walks out to her car, wondering what Zion will do when he sees her. "It's been a long time, and the Champagne is no longer available. What should I say? What should I do?" she sighs. "Just be there to listen and comfort him," Zena tells herself as she drives back to her hotel.

≈

Carlito Lopez, Corrin's husband, and a very successful pharmaceutical executive, is overjoyed to have her back. Because of their jobs, the couple has to spend a lot of time apart.

Corrin walks into the master bathroom and sees that Carlito has made a milk bubble bath with rose petals. The steam from the bath gives the room a calming, flowery smell. Corrin quickly strips off her clothes and slides into the warm, luscious liquid that fills her enormous marble tub.

"This is perfect timing for me. Oh, honey, you care for me so tenderly."

Carlito walks into the restroom and says, "When you give me the chance, I try." His first natural reaction is to take a deep breath. "I hope we can start a family soon, Corrin. We're in good health, mentally and physically, and we have a comfortable income. We're both getting older, and I think you'd make a wonderful mother. With each passing day, we lose the chance to bring our love into the world as a new life. Just imagine all the laughs we'll have attempting to conceive a child, whether a boy or a girl."

Corrin rolls her eyes and looks away from her husband. "This was supposed to be a relaxing bath, right? Do we have to talk about starting a family as soon as I get home? Join me and in the morning and we can talk about babies."

Carlito agrees to do as his wife asks.

CHAPTER THREE

All That Jazmine

"WELCOME TO TOPAZ, WHERE WE bring out your inner gem. One of our professional staff members will be with you shortly. Would you like a pomegranate mimosa?" Jazmine inquires of her first clients of the day.

"Sure," the ladies all say at once.

Jazmine has the entrepreneurial tenacity of her father and has annihilated her competitors. Hers is the leading full-service salon serving Delmarva and the Eastern Shore. Topaz's professional staff includes hair stylists, spa staff, manicurists, facial specialists, hair colorists, and certified hair extension experts. Her third salon has already filled up all their slots nine months in advance.

"Daddy, what are you doing here?" she asks, smiling broadly and hugging Zion.

"How could I miss the grand opening of my daughter's latest location? I'm extremely proud of you. Lovebug, you're doing great things."

"Thank you very much! But don't you think I'm too old to be referred to as Lovebug?"

"Never! You will always be my Lovebug."

"Daddy, please stop embarrassing me in front of my clients," Jazmine pouts.

"Girl, let your dad love on you. At least he is present. Some of us wish we had a dad. If you do not wish to keep him, I will!" one of her customers exclaims.

Jazmine playfully taunts, "He's not for sale, thank you," and the laughter of her customers fills the room.

"I'm leaving, I'm leaving, so you ladies can return to your beauty regimen and my daughter can return to her job," says Zion. "I love you. Until then, Jazzy." Zion embraces Jazmine once more before leaving.

"Thanks a lot for coming, Dad. I appreciate it and love you, too."

While Zion is leaving, Jazmine's long-time fiancé, Adrian Johnson, is walking in.

"Adrian," Zion says as he nods his head.

"What's happening, Mr. Spencer? Long time no see."

After hearing this, Zion mutters, "Not long enough," as he continues to walk toward his car.

Rejecting Zion's snide remark, Adrian continues to walk. "This is a great day for your business. You can shake that moneymaker for me after you've made some dough from this." He says this as he reaches around and kisses the back of Jazmine's neck.

"Honey, don't do that in front of the clients. Be respectful of my workplace, thanks! " Jazmine exclaims as she wrenches herself away from his grip.

"Oh, that's how it is now. A nigga shows up and tries to support your bougie ass and this is the thanks I get. I'm outta here!"

"Adrian! Adrian, wait!" Jazmine shouts, but Adrian storms out of the salon.

For the inconvenience, Jazmine is giving all of her customers a ten percent discount as an apology.

For a long time, Adrian has been an annoyance to Zion. Since he lacks a formal education, he has worked at a wide variety of temporary jobs. Besides his criminal history, the fact that he has three children from two different women disqualifies him as a potential husband for Zion's precious daughter. Adrian would gladly take your underwear if he had the chance.

Zion believes Jazmine is more attracted to Adrian out of lust than out of love. He's tall, handsome, and charming with a rough, bad-boy air. His sexcalibur led to the nickname "Meatman" becoming popular. Champagne is probably turning in her grave knowing that her beloved daughter is dating a man who is neither her superior nor equal in terms of wealth. The only consideration in all of Adrian's decisions, though, is Jazmine.

Keeping her happy is his top priority. He loves her, but most of all he loves the lifestyle being with her affords him, which is what disgusts Zion. The truth may be hidden from Jazmine, but it is clear to her father. Zion tried to give Jazmine a clue about her Bozo not being her Boaz. Unfortunately, it backfired, and Jazmine did not speak to her father for three months. Since that incident, Zion refrains from acknowledging the relationship.

After hours at the salon, Jazmine is finally home and ready to relax from her exhausting day. She walks up the long slate path and opens the big mahogany front door, where she can smell a home-cooked meal.

Jazmine calls, "Babe."

"I'm in the dining room," Adrian responds. The table is elegantly set with candles, roses, stemware, and china. Adrian pulls out a chair and says, "Please take a seat. Dinner is served, my love. Smothered pork chops, mashed potatoes, and a Caesar salad are on the menu. I almost forgot about the dinner rolls."

Adrian dashes into the kitchen and takes them out of the oven. "Ouch!" Jazmine snickers as she hears the baking sheet hit the counter.

Adrian reappears, carrying butter and rolls in a glass dish. He pours red wine into a glass and takes a seat next to Jazmine. "I apologize for my earlier outburst, baby. You did not deserve it. I know you're a professional, but whenever I see your fine ass, I can't keep my hands off you. But that's no excuse, and I apologize if I embarrassed you in front of your customers. I'm going to be more formal. Are we good?" Adrian inquires.

"Yes, but not as good as these pork chops. You put your foot in this gravy. This was right on time. I didn't eat lunch, and I'm starving. You're forgiven. We need to have apology dinners more often," responds Jazmine, devouring a bite of her pork chop.

Adrian licks the gravy from the bottom of Jazmine's lip. "This meal isn't the only item on the menu tonight."

"Stop it. Do not start. I'm hungry, tired, and need a shower."

"It's all right, Ma. Finish your meal. I'll start your bath and bring dessert to your room." Adrian massages her shoulders.

"Mmm, that feels so good. This is the best apology massage. I love you."

"You're so tight. I must stretch you out. Loosen you up a bit. Would you like that?" asks Adrian.

"Indeed," replies Jazmine, and she finishes her dinner.

Lavender and honey scent Adrian's master bathroom, where he stands like a Nubian king with a soft cream bath towel wrapped around his hips. Jazmine bites her bottom lip, taking in the sight of her man as he confronts her. He undresses the beautiful, curvy, plus-size diva while staring into her eyes.

"Jazz, it's all about you. I'll devote the rest of my life to you."

Adrian takes Jazmine's hand and leads her to the bathtub after they kiss passionately for what feels like several minutes. She immerses herself in the warm water, resting her head on the bath pillow. Adrian lathers up a bath loofah with honey-scented body wash and begins bathing his future bride.

Adrian massages sensual oils across every inch of his lover's body after her bath, his magic touch lulling her to sleep. Adrian, disappointed that he cannot get his freak on, covers the exhausted sleeping beauty, grabs the sensual oil, and strokes his third leg until he falls asleep next to her.

CHAPTER FOUR

Dashing Dexter

P EOPLE KNOW DEXTER, OR DEX for short, as the only boy in his family, and they appreciate his easygoing nature, sense of humor, and generous heart. Dexter, the youngest and the one least affected by Champagne's venom, clung to Mother Gayle Spencer and was now making a successful business out of playing laser tag and video games. To gather information about what he hopes will be the best possible family vacation spot, he visits Japan, Brazil, and many American cities. Since opening, TNT has seen tremendous success; its second location, which also features a skating rink and bowling lanes, is doing even better. Dexter has found success as a businessman and is happy about it. He is a fine example of a single man; like his father, he has a way with the ladies and is yet to tie the knot. Dex stands at an impressive five feet ten inches and has a slender and muscular physique. He has a latte complexion and deep brown eyes that complement his thick, curly, sandy-brown hair. At Dex's second TNT outpost, he gets an unexpected visitor.

"Greetings, stranger," a tiny but mighty voice says.

"Grandma!" Dex jumps up from his desk and exclaims as he approaches her.

"You've been working so much that I don't get to see you very often. You remind me of your father; working too hard," says Mother Spencer.

Dexter kisses her on the cheek and says, "I've missed you and your home-cooked meals. I'm busy with my businesses, but I enjoy what I do. What brought you here?"

"Do I require a reason to visit my favorite grandson?"

"I'm the only grandson you have."

"That's why I like you best!" Both laugh out loud.

"What am I going to do with you, Grandma?"

"Nothing. I'm an old woman with set habits. Give me another hug and some sugar. I'm about to get out of your hair." Dex hugs his grandmother and kisses her on the cheek once more.

"Grandmother, I love you. You are welcome to visit. Choose a date and I'll take you to dinner."

"I'm going to hold you to that," Mother Spencer says as she walks toward the door.

"Okay. See you later."

"Bye, baby."

When Mother Spencer is on her way to her car, she hears, "What are you doing here?"

"Why are you being nosy, Zion?"

"Momma, you're always on the road. Do you ever sit still?"

"No. I can be still when I'm dead. If I have breath in my body and use of my limbs, I'm going to go until I can't go anymore. If you must know, I was visiting my handsome grandson."

"I'm here to see Dex as well."

"You two have an enjoyable time. I'm on my way to visit one sister from the church. Mother Odell has been ill. I'm going to go see her. I made her a pot of chicken noodle soup. I'm a go on now so the soup isn't ice cold by the time I get to her," Mother Spencer says as she hugs Zion.

"All right, Momma. Drive safely and I'll talk to you later," Zion says as he enters TNT.

"Dad, you just missed Grandma," Dexter says.

"I caught her in the parking lot."

"It's been a family affair today. What brings you by?"

"Well, son, I'm trying to impress a few young tech millionaires I'm meeting at the end of this week. I was wondering if we could get the VIP treatment. This could help me seal the investment deal of the quarter."

"I will ensure you all are given the royal treatment from the time you arrive until you leave."

"The possibilities could be endless. Son, I appreciate this. Are you going to be home for dinner tonight?" asks Zion.

"I doubt it. I have a few things to finish at work."

"One other thing," Zion says, holding Dex's gaze, "you're an adult. However, can you limit the number of different young ladies you bring into my house?" When Dexter raises his eyebrows, Zion continues, "I get it. You're a nice-looking guy with some money. You work hard and want to play hard. The ladies love you—but don't lose the love for yourself. I don't know what you're chasing or looking for, but you won't find it in the sheets. I wasted a lot of years looking for something that I would've seen I already had if I'd just opened my eyes. Please don't repeat my mistakes. Learn from them. Your professional life is thriving, so evaluate your personal life. You're getting older, and I'd like grandchildren before we're both in diapers. You hear me, son?"

"Yes, sir."

"I love you."

"I love you, too, Dad."

CHAPTER FIVE

Sahara and No-Action Jackson

"**I**s this where I sign paperwork for investing?" asks a stranger who is a tall, bald, dark-brown brother in the middle of her presentation to potential clients.

She collects herself quickly enough to say, "Sir, see the information specialist at the desk in the middle of the hall."

"Thank you, beautiful," replies the gentleman as he closes the conference room door.

Sahara has just finished her presentation to the upper and middle management executives when the same man from earlier stops her on her way back to her office.

"Miss, I'm sorry for interrupting your meeting. My name's Jackson. Jackson Andrews. Who do I have the pleasure of meeting today?"

"A very busy woman," she says as she departs.

"Wait, wait, wait! You can't leave me standing here without letting me know your name."

"Watch me," Sahara says as she makes her way to her office.

"Hold on, lovely. I'll be here every day until I find out what your name is," Jackson responds as he walks quickly behind Sahara.

"So you're not only stalking me, but you also don't have a job? You cannot post here and work at the same time," Sahara responds sarcastically.

"I own a small business. I can come here as much as I want and still make money. Tell me your name if you don't want to see my face again—though I'm sure you do."

"Rumpelstiltskin," Sahara says as she walks into her office and shuts the door firmly.

Jackson smiles as he reads aloud "Sahara Patterson" in front of the door.

"Dammit, the door," Sahara mumbles to herself.

The next day, when Sahara comes back from a meeting, she finds he has sent two dozen red roses to her office. According to the card: "Rumpelstiltskin, let's continue our conversation over dinner. I'll see you at six p.m. at Indulge. Jackson." Sahara chuckles and agrees to meet him for dinner.

As Sahara enters the restaurant, the maître d' leads her to a private table with lovely, crisp white linens. They set the table with crystal glasses of various sizes and heights, fine china, and silverware.

Jackson stands; his knees feel like jello from the sight of Sahara approaching him. As she sits, he pushes her chair in. "I didn't think you'd show up tonight," he says as he takes his seat.

I didn't want to give in, but between your insistence and my hunger, it was a no-brainer.

"Oh, cupid shot an arrow through my heart," says Jackson, holding his chest.

"Stop it! I'm sure your mother taught you how to behave properly in a restaurant. Thank you for the roses, by the way. They were lovely."

"You're very welcome. You have a beautiful smile. I'd like to wake up every morning to that smile for the rest of my life," Jackson asserts.

"You don't even know who I am."

"That's why we're having dinner tonight. There will hopefully be many more dinners to come."

"Why did you invite me out? There were a lot of women in the office."

"As you gave your presentation, I watched you through the glass. You had complete command of the attention of everyone in the room. My heart melted and I fell to my feet when you smiled at them. I knew then that I had to at least speak with you. You're both beautiful and intelligent. Talk about a complete package," Jackson explains.

"I am a complete package. I have a child."

"I love kids, and they love me."

"Do you have an answer for everything?" Sahara inquires.

"Almost everything. I have yet to find the right woman with whom to have children. In my spirit, I sense a shift has occurred."

"That could be gas," Sahara jokes.

Jackson and Sahara enjoy their dinner, which is full of laughter and intelligent conversation.

≈

A couple of weeks later, Sahara sees Jackson at her place of employment again. He is hugging a woman, and Sahara cannot see her face. When Jackson notices Sahara watching him, he takes the woman by the hand and walks toward Sahara.

"Hello there, Sahara. How are things going for you today?" Ms. Maybell inquires.

"Ma'am, I'm fine. I did not know you knew Jackson."

"Now it makes sense," Ms. Maybell says. "You're the lovely lady my son has been telling me about."

"I've known you for years and had no idea you had a son."

"He is my only child. He's a hard worker who isn't bothered by baby-momma drama."

"Momma, you're talking about me as if I'm not standing next to you," Jackson says.

"Children, regardless of age, should only be seen and not heard. Adults are speaking," his mother retorts, and the three of them burst out laughing.

Sahara and Jackson talk on the phone all the time, go on multiple dates each week, and include Milah. Sahara and Jackson elope six months later, against her parents' and Mother Spencer's wishes.

He moves into her house and turns one bedroom into his office, deciding to rent out his three-bedroom, two-and-a-half-bath traditional ranch for extra income. Four months have passed, and the newlyweds have planned a family barbecue to commemorate their marriage. While Milah assists her mother and stepfather in bringing food outside to grill, Mother Spencer and Zion arrive first, entering the backyard through the fence.

"Daddy! Mom-Mom! I'm so glad you could attend," as she hugs them, Sahara says.

"We love you, and I pray for you every day," Mother Spencer says.

"Where is the man who abducted my daughter, robbing me of the chance to walk her down the aisle?"

Jackson approaches them quickly after placing a pan of hot dogs fresh off the grill on a table. "Mr. Spencer, good to see you, sir," Jackson says as he extends his hand to Zion.

"Let's go for a walk, son," Zion says, looking at his hand. Jackson agrees, and the two men walk away.

"I'm hoping Daddy isn't too harsh on him."

"Your father is very protective of you. Allow him to say his piece. What were you thinking, running away and getting married without telling us?"

"I'm an adult, and we're in a relationship. Isn't marriage preferable to burning?" Sahara inquires.

"Don't you dare twist Scripture to suit your purposes! I'm not sure how I feel about this. We want you to be truly happy. That isn't the problem. What information do you have about this man and his family? How does he assist you and Milah?"

"I wasn't trying to be disrespectful, Mom-Mom. His parents are middle-class working professionals. Jackson's e-commerce businesses provide him with multiple revenue streams. He pays all the bills and adores Milah as if she were his own flesh and blood. What more could I want in a husband?" Sahara wonders.

"The Lord has given me a powerful discernment spirit," Mother Spencer says. "He has a good heart, but something isn't quite right. Just know that I'm available to you whenever you need me. Dominique and Demetrius would cancel their African mission trip if they were aware of this."

"That is why I have not informed them. Dad has always wanted to preach the gospel in Africa, and Mom is making international business connections. I'll inform them when the time comes," Sahara makes a promise.

"You better—or I will," warns Mother Spencer.

"Yes, ma'am," Sahara responds as the two women fix their gaze on Zion and Jackson.

"Mr. Spencer, may I address you as Dad? We've become family."

"No. What do you want with my daughter?"

"I'm in love with her. I want to bring joy to her life for the rest of her days."

"Cut the nonsense! My daughter is a good girl, a caring mother, and a hard worker. Her only flaw is that she has a big heart, which causes her to miss obvious things. I did my research on you. Your businesses are losing thousands of dollars each month because of your risky business practices, lack of strategic planning, and lack of development. The mortgage on the house you've been renting is two months late. I'm guessing you've kept my daughter in the dark about your financial difficulties. Did you marry my daughter to profit from the fact that I was her father?" Zion inquires, disgusted.

"No, sir. I truly love your daughter. We're both businessmen, you and me. You understand we must take colossal risks in order to reap big rewards. It's just the way the beast is. I did not know you were her father until we eloped. However, I am offended that you would investigate me behind my back. I'm a walking manifesto. If you had given me the chance, I would have shown you my financial situation. This is something I can fix. My goal is not to worry Sahara. I'm going to do everything I can to keep this family together and moving forward," Jackson responds.

"You have sixty days to turn around your businesses. If nothing happens, Jackson, I'll swoop in and save the day, doing whatever I can to get you out of my daughter's life for good. Are we on the same page, son?"

"Yes, sir," Jackson responds, and the two men return to Sahara and Mother Spencer.

"Did you boys have a pleasant talk?" Mother Spencer inquires.

"Yes, Momma, we did. I believe we have a good understanding of our responsibilities. Isn't that correct, Jackson?"

"We have, sir. I value our one-on-one conversation. I hope to see many more in the future," Jackson responds in the same way.

Guests with covered dishes enter the backyard.

"Hey, let's have a party over here! Where am I going to put this?" Jazmine yells as she approaches Sahara, carrying a roaster pan full of pasta salad.

"There are tables and coolers over there," Sahara responds, pointing to the right.

"I haven't been here in a long time. Your house is adorable. But

I could never live in a house smaller than three thousand square feet," Jazmine makes a snide remark.

"Hello, hello," Corrin says as she walks through the gate into the backyard. "I brought hand sanitizer and a bowl of mixed summer fruits."

"Thank you very much, Corrin. I wasn't sure if you'd be able to make it with your hectic schedule," Sahara exclaims with glee.

"I take breaks from time to time to mingle with the commoners. Isn't your house charming? Hmm," remarks Corrin.

"My girl is not a breastfed, trust-fund princess. Sahara earned what she has by working hard and refusing help from three parents, not to mention while being a single parent. She is one of the strongest, most self-sufficient women I know and deserves a lot of respect," Rwanda, Sahara's best friend, declares as she examines her stuck-up half-siblings. "What's on the menu, girlfriend?" Rwanda asks, taking Sahara by the arm and leaving her sisters perplexed.

"I can't stand those bougie-ass babes!" Rwanda exclaims when she and Sahara are out of earshot. "Who needs enemies when you have sisters like that? Damn! Why do you put up with so much nonsense from them? They insult and denigrate you. I believe it hardens their nipples."

"He may not appear when you want Him to, but you were on time. My sista, you arrived on time," Sahara explains.

"I didn't want to talk to their asses, but when I heard how they were speaking to you, Sahara, I couldn't take it anymore."

"For the most part, I ignore their remarks. They blame me for their mother's death and everything wrong in the world, though neither of them has ever admitted it. But if Daddy hadn't been protecting me, their mother might still be here."

"But then *you* wouldn't be. Let me tell you something. Their mother was insane. You were a child and had nothing to do with Champagne's actions. She got a gun on her own and tried to kill you. That's the nonsense your sisters refuse to admit. You cannot change your birth circumstances. That was not your fault. It has been two decades since her death. Stop giving your sisters a pass to dis-serve you because you feel guilty about your mother's affair with their father. It's wrong on so many levels! You're a good person, and no one deserves to be limited by their parents' sins," Rwanda vented.

"You're right," Sahara agrees.

"I mistook this for a party. Let's get this party started!" Rwanda declares.

CHAPTER SIX

Hiding in Plain Sight

ORRIN SITS IN HER FEMININE office. She decorated the elaborate pink and white space with one-of-a-kind rose-gold fixtures and lighting, and her logo is hand-painted on the wall behind her desk.

She smiles as she remembers her mother, and an idea occurs to her. Corrin takes out her phone. "Is Ms. Zena Whitcomb available this morning? Corrin Spencer-Lopez here."

"Hello, precious, this is Zena…and please call me Auntie Z."

"All right," Corrin says.

"How has your day gone so far?"

"It's fine. Today I've been thinking a lot about my mother. When I reach personal goals, it is at those times that I miss her the most. I wish she could see the woman I've become because of her teaching and mentoring."

"I'm sure your mother sees and knows everything you've done, and she couldn't be more proud of you. Your mother told me she named you after the Bible's book of Corinthians because you represent the right and perfect love she had for your father. Corinth was a prosperous and bustling city. It exercised dominance over land access from east to west. That's why you're such a successful business owner. It's written in your name. His words cannot be returned void."

"It will accomplish what it is sent out to do," the ladies agree.

"It's been a pleasure speaking with you, Auntie Z. You appear to have been very close to my mother. You carry a piece of her spirit with you. I'd appreciate it if you could join my family and I for dinner tonight. I'm going to introduce you to Jazmine and Dexter. Are you available tonight? I know it's short notice, but I think they'll enjoy hearing all about Momma. What do you think?" Corrin inquires, eagerly awaiting a response.

"All right. Please text me your address. I'd love to meet you all for dinner."

"I'll call Dad and see if he can come with us. He rarely mentions Momma. I believe it is too painful for him. Wonderful memories of Momma will help his soul. I'll text you as soon as we finish talking. Thank you very much," Corrin continues.

"For what?" asks Auntie Z.

"Because you were exactly what I needed right now. Auntie Z, I'll see you later." Corrin is too excited to plan the menu for tonight's dinner.

≈

"Do you think having dinner with them would be a good idea? It's taken you a long time to get here," Zena's longtime nurse and friend, Judith, agrees. "I believe you are moving too quickly. You're a medical marvel. So far, the experimental procedures and drugs have been effective, but you cannot afford a medical setback."

"My father spent millions of dollars to save me from certain death. When I awoke from my six-year coma, it felt like someone had kicked me in the gut. I was in a foreign country with strangers all around me. Everything had changed, but time had stopped for me, and I longed to be reunited with my family. You know I couldn't walk or talk for three years because of experimental medical treatments.

Zena continues, "After eleven years—eleven years, Judith—I left Switzerland and moved to London, on my own for the first time in my life—thanks to Daddy for setting up a trust and providing me with a whole new identity to go with my new life—but now, with him and Mother both deceased, I'm completely alone, which is ridiculous. I have a family. Twenty years have passed; haven't I lost enough time? The coma, surgeries, treatments in multiple countries, rehabilitation, and speech therapy all led to this point. I am as prepared as I can be. I have yearned to see my beloved Zion and children."

"Corrin didn't recognize me—"

"Why should she? I'm only half the woman I once was, and the plastic surgeon did an excellent job on my face. Judith, I promise I'll leave immediately if I become overwhelmed," Zena says.

"Champagne, I'd like to state unequivocally that I do not believe this is a clever idea."

"It's been years since anyone even mentioned my name. Don't use that phrase in front of me. She is dead!"

"OK, but call me if you get into any trouble," Judith responds.

As she prepares for an evening with her family, Zena nods in agreement.

≈

"Dammit! What's the deal with this idiot oven?" Corrin yells. Her phone rings as she is preparing dinner for tonight. "Hello?"

"Hello, princess. I apologize for taking so long to return your call. What's the deal with dinner?"

"Dad, I invited Zena Whitcomb, one of Momma's close friends, over for dinner tonight. But there's a problem with my oven. I may have to reschedule."

"No. Don't cancel on her. You are welcome to have dinner at my home. It'll be like old times with all of my children together. We're all so busy. I rarely see you together. You can fill me in on what I've been missing in your lives," says Zion.

"Do you consider Sahara to be one of your children?" Corrin inquires, her disgust visible.

"She is my daughter and your sister, but tonight is Sahara and Jackson's weekly family night. They won't be able to come to dinner with us."

"Oh, what a shame," Corrin quips sarcastically.

"You two need to work things out. I expect more from you, Corrin, as the oldest. Isn't there something in the Bible about having an ought against your brother—or sister—in your case?"

"Sir, yes."

"Then repair it! I'm tired of playing referee between you two. Mother Spencer is on her way to my house, bringing new tablecloths. Perhaps she can assist you in preparing your dinner. I'll see you soon. I love you," Zion says.

"I love you, Dad, and thank you."

Thank God for small mercies! The last thing I want to do is share pleasant memories of my mother with her murderer, Corrin thinks to herself as she hangs up the phone.

Corrin understands Sahara was too young to be directly involved in her mother's death. She does, however, blame Sahara for her mother's loss of sanity during her mother's last hours on Earth. Corrin believes

Sahara is as guilty as if she had pulled the trigger herself. Corrin shakes her head, attempting to refocus her attention on dinner tonight.

The aroma of food cooking wafts outside her father's house, tantalizing her taste buds. Corrin opens the door to find Mother Spencer doing what she does best: cooking.

"Mom-Mom, good evening."

"Baby, come on in. Your father told me everything about your special dinner tonight. He also mentioned that you were having problems with your oven. I hope you don't mind an old goat assisting you."

"You saved my skin if by GOAT you mean the greatest of all time. What is it that smells so divine?"

"Brown sugar and Cajun-seasoned Cornish hens, red-skinned mashed potatoes, a garden salad, and homemade yeast rolls with cinnamon butter are on the menu. The red velvet cake is cooling on the rack, and the cream cheese frosting is chilling in the fridge. We can both ice the cake in about twenty minutes. You can decide what you all want to drink," Mother Spencer says.

Corrin wraps her arms around her grandmother.

"Are you okay?" Mother Spencer inquires.

"Tonight was supposed to be perfect, but obstacles were popping up like popcorn. You've been such a help. Mom-Mom, I can't thank you enough. Dad said you were bringing new dining table linens. May I inspect them?"

"When you were young, I promised you I would always be there for you, and I meant it. I know you're a successful young woman now, but you'll always be my baby. Now, set the table. The linens are in the box in the buffet's corner. I believe you'll enjoy this set in particular," Mother Spencer says as she removes the browned hens from the oven.

Corrin removes the box's cover, revealing gray, gold, and cream linens that complement the gold-trimmed china.

"Yes! Thank you, Jesus!" Corrin exclaims from the dining room.

"By your response, I assume I can stamp your approval on my linen selection?"

"Yes, ma'am. A triple stamp."

When Dex and Jazz arrive shortly after their father, Corrin is finishing up the table setting by adding fresh flowers. Zion embraces and kisses each of his children.

"Pop, you're acting as if you haven't seen me in months. It's only been a couple of days. I'm not into all this sentimentality," Dexter says.

"You keep quiet and let your father spoil you. God knows you've had enough young women trying to love you long time," Mother Spencer teases, and the family bursts out laughing.

"Did Grandma just come for me?" jokes Dex.

"Boom! She did, indeed. Say something else now. I thought so," Jazmine exclaims.

"Who is this woman, Corrin, this Zena?" Dexter inquires.

"So, what makes her so unique? You've got Mom-Mom over here preparing all of this food. She's getting too old to do all of this," Jazmine adds.

"I won't be old until I'm cold. Corrin didn't ask, so I offered to assist her, but I'm going to leave before your company arrives. Have fun and enjoy the food. It warms my heart to see everyone laughing and smiling. This family has been through a lot, but by God's grace, we are still alive. I love each and every one of you. Corrin, please call and let me know how you're doing tonight. Do you hear me?" Mother Spencer inquires.

"Yes, ma'am."

"We love you, too. Drive safe," the family shouts as Mother Spencer walks to the door. The doorbell rings just as she is about to open it.

"Hello there; you must be Zena," Mother Spencer says as she opens the door. "Corrin has said nice things about you." She reaches out to shake Zena's hand.

Champagne's surprise at seeing Mother Spencer causes her to become temporarily paralyzed as she remembers the pictures from the Spencer barbecue so many years ago. She regains her composure as her transfixed position makes everyone uncomfortable for Mother Spencer.

"I'm truly sorry. The kids have grown a lot since I last saw them. You're all grown up now. I don't think I'm as ready to see you as I thought I was." Zena finally shakes Mother Spencer's hand.

Mother Spencer searches Zena's eyes for the secret she is hiding in plain sight. "Don't worry about it," she says. "Some of us have had a long day; longer than others. Have a nice night."

"Come on in, Zena. I'll take your jacket," Corrin invites.

Mother Spencer stands there until the front door shuts. She detects darkness within Zena and decides to keep a close eye on her. Meanwhile, the Spencer's and their visitor have taken their seats at the dining room table, with Corrin placing Zena next to her father.

"Please allow me to introduce you to my family, Zena. My sister, Jazmine, and brother, Dexter, are sitting in front of you, and my father, Zion, is sitting next to you."

"Thank you all for your kindness. Please call me Auntie Z now that we've gotten the formalities out of the way."

Corrin and Jazmine agree to do as she requests, and they place the food on top of the buffet in the dining room.

"Could you please bless the food, Dad?"

"Of course. Heavenly Father, thank you for this food, and bless the hands that prepared it. Thank you for the opportunity to be in the presence of my children whom I love with all my heart. Thank you for sending Zena here safely. Thank you for this food we are about to receive. Bless it as nourishment for our bodies. Amen."

"I thought you were going to take us to church, Daddy."

"You're the eternal jokester, Jazzy," Zion responds, and everyone laughs as Corrin and Jazmine remove the food from the buffet and begin scooping servings onto everyone's plates.

"Every man for himself if you want seconds," Jazmine says as she and Corrin take their seats at the table.

"I'm sorry, Zena, but I've been racking my brain trying to remember you. My memory has suffered because of the passage of time," Zion says.

"They haven't taken a toll on the rest of you," Zena slyly observes. "It's fine. Champagne and I talked mostly on the phone. I was one of her former private school classmates."

"I've got you. That clarifies things," Zion responds.

His children exchange glances, noticing their father missed Zena's mildly flirtatious remark.

"Have you settled into your new place yet, Zena?" Corrin inquires.

"I'm making progress. I still need to pick up a few pieces of furniture."

"Guys, I have a fantastic idea! We have a lot of Momma's belongings in storage. Would you like to pick out a few things for your condo since you two were so close? As a tribute to Momma and a thank you for all your kind words? Is there anyone who objects to this?" Corrin inquires.

"No; I think it's a fantastic idea. Your mother had great taste. It would be nice if someone close to her could enjoy the things she enjoyed," Zion says.

"Yes, my dear. Momma had great taste. She made sure we were always dressed to impress," Jazmine concurs.

"I despised those neckties," Dexter says with a shake of his head, adding, "but I'm cool. Take whatever you want."

Throughout the evening, the Spencer's and Zena share their fondest memories and most amusing stories about Champagne.

"This has been a fantastic evening. I'm overwhelmed by your generosity and hospitality," Zena says.

"Dad, I think it'd be a friendly gesture for you to give Zena a personal tour of the area now that she's reacquainted with it. Delaware has transformed over the years," Corrin explains.

"That is correct. A newcomer could easily get lost here. You could end up in the middle of nowhere if you take the wrong turn," Jazmine adds.

"Girls, don't put any pressure on your father. He's a man on the go. I wouldn't want to interfere with his plans," Zena responds.

Jazmine quips, "He needs to get out more," with mocking humor.

Zion breathes out loud. "Girls, I absolutely love what I do. I'm kept busy and away from trouble by it. Zena, I'm sorry about my overprotective daughters. I sincerely hope you're not ashamed."

"I'm not, no. They clearly love their father, as I can see."

Zion says, "Well, I'm embarrassed. But I'd be glad to show you around my town if you'd like. I haven't had a good excuse to take a day off in a while."

Zena says, "Thank you. That'll be wonderful. I've spent a lot of time alone. Getting outside will be beneficial to me as well. My business card is here. Call me so that we can discuss our schedules."

Accepting the card, Zion tucks it inside his blazer's inner pocket. "That seems like a plan."

"It sounds like a date," his daughters say as they turn to face their brother and then each other.

"That's all, young ladies. Thank you for providing dinner. I'll go upstairs. Girls, put your energy to good use by cleaning up. Again, Zena, it was a pleasure to meet you. Good night, children," Zion says as he walks upstairs to his room.

CHAPTER SEVEN

Family Dynamics

CHAMPAGNE AND ZION'S CHILDREN ARE all successful business owners, according to all accounts. They are well-educated and live in luxurious homes within gated communities, whereas Sahara, their half-sister, is a college dropout who was a single parent before marrying Jackson.

Mother Spencer decides to cook a feast for her son and grandchildren after a few weeks have passed since Zena's visit. Corrin and Jazmine both show up with their significant others at the same time. Dexter shows up with his current Miss Right Now about ten minutes later. The Spencer's congregate in the family room.

"Mom, it smells wonderful in here. I'm all set to eat. Is everyone present?"

"You know we're always waiting for your daughter," Corrin states sarcastically.

"Your younger sister is on her way home from work, and you know she has a family of her own. They'll be here soon, I'm sure. Why don't you practice expressing some of the good Lord's compassion in your sermons?" Mother Spencer responds.

"I'm parched. Please excuse me." Corrin struts toward the wet bar, her eyes rolling.

Mother Spencer always has Sahara's back, Corrin thinks to herself as she peers across the room at her family.

Corrin and Jazmine are convinced that Mother Spencer prefers Sahara over them. What they don't realize is the Holy Spirit leads and guides Mother Spencer. She has always known how badly the sisters have treated Sahara, and her constant prayer is that the girls will free themselves from the demonic lie spoon-fed to them by their late mother. Their grandmother recognizes the sisters have memorialized their mother as someone she never was and that they have endured countless family members' re-tellings of their father's undying love for his childhood sweetheart, Dominique. Champagne has always been portrayed as the second best to the one who escaped Zion's grasp.

Dexter was never susceptible to hearsay or rumors. He kept close to Mother Spencer, plate in hand, eagerly awaiting her next best dish. Dex knows his parents loved each other and him, and in his world, that is all that matters. He enjoys having Sahara as a younger sibling and has grown to admire her. He has witnessed firsthand Corrin and Jazmine's petty, relentless attacks on Sahara and despises their treatment of her, but Dex only intervenes when Sahara is about to snap.

"Hello, hello, everyone. "We apologize for being late, Daddy," Sahara says as she walks in with her husband. She wraps her arms around her father and kisses him on the cheek.

"Where is my hug, sis?" Dex says as he extends his arms toward Sahara.

"You know I'll always be there with a hug for you, bro. I looooove you."

"I looooove you even more."

"Hello, Jazz. What happened to Corrin?"

Jazmine raises her hand and says, "Hey."

Corrin enters the family room after hearing the commotion and concluding that Sahara has arrived.

"Hello, big sis," Sahara says. "I was just wondering how you were."

"What do you want with me?"

"Sahara, Mother Spencer has spent the entire day cooking on Dad's stove, and I'm starving! Are you not? Let's all go to the dining room." While Mother Spencer scowls at Corrin, Dexter shifts the conversation's focus.

"God is watching," Corrin's grandmother says as she walks past her.

Jackson retrieves Sahara's dinner chair.

"You're still in the honeymoon stage. It must be wonderful to be a father," Carlito tells Jackson.

"There's nothing like it anywhere in the world, man. Sahara has enriched my life in so many ways. Every day, I thank God for this wonderful woman," Jackson responds.

Adrian, not to be outdone, says, "I've also been a fortunate man. I'm not sure where I'd be if it weren't for my Jazzy Boo's love and patience. Jazz took her time and poured her love into me when all I knew was the streets. Now I'm sitting here, a changed man. You understand what I am saying. We're living the life, baby!"

Zion, unimpressed by both of his daughters' suitors, says, "I raised ladies, not babies. Because I told them they were winners, my daughters are winners. I showed them how to become the head rather than the tail. Because of this, they can all survive with or without a man." Zion takes a forkful of food and places it in his mouth.

"We Spencer women are one-of-a-kind," Sahara emphasizes.

"How could you possibly know? Are you not a Patterson?" Jazmine inquires angrily.

"Her name is Mrs. Andrews," Jackson responds.

"What does her name have to do with the fact that she's a Spencer?" exclaims Zion. "My blood flows through her veins just as it does through your siblings'. I'm tired of your disdain and contempt for your sister. That's correct! Sahara is your damn sister! It's about time you started treating her like it! Your snide remarks will come to an end tonight! How dare you act like this in my home! I'll cut you and Corrin out of my will if you and Corrin don't respect Sahara as a member of this family. I have said nothing in years, hoping you'd grow out of it and work it out among yourselves. Enough already! Do you want to be remembered as your mother? Hatred drove her insane!"

"How can you talk about our mother in this way, especially in front of her? You've chosen her over your first family once more!" Corrin screams.

"There is no such thing as a first or second family. You're all my kids. I love you and will protect you, even if it means protecting you from yourself. I think you and Jazmine should leave right now," Zion asserts.

"I'll leave, Daddy. I don't want to cause any more problems," Sahara announces softly.

"Too late, boo," Jazmine says.

"That's it!" Zion smolders. "Leave right now!"

"Father, are you telling us to leave the family home where we grew up?" Corrin wonders. "Where our mother raised us until her untimely death?"

"You don't quit while you're ahead, Corrin," Zion says. "No, you must turn the knife slightly deeper. The more I believe you've matured naturally and spiritually, the more I see your mother's behaviors—the ones that took her life—reflected in you. Before destruction, there is a warning. Get off the road you're on. I'm afraid it will not end well for you. I'm getting older and tired. I desire peace, particularly in my home. I'm done with this discussion. Good evening." Zion then takes his plate and goes upstairs to his room.

Corrin and Jazmine walk away quietly with their companions, their gaze fixed on Sahara the entire time.

When the front door slams shut, Sahara sobs uncontrollably as Jackson tries to comfort her.

Dexter, to console his younger sister, says, "It's not your fault. You did an excellent job, as usual, of ignoring their comments. Dad's candor surprised me. He said exactly what we've been thinking for years. My sisters are wonderful, but they can be genuine witches. Are you okay, Sahara?"

"Yes. I just wish there wasn't so much squabbling. I can't change who I was born to be. How do I apologize for simply existing? I didn't ask to be here, but I'm here, making the best of an unpleasant situation."

"You're not an unpleasant situation. The only way to put the devil on the run is with prayer," says Mother Spencer. "Father God, I come to you in the name of Jesus, as your humble servant, to intercede for my son and grandchildren. Cool their tempers, touch their minds, and instill in them a spirit of peace and forgiveness. You predetermined all of our births. You were familiar with our parents as well as the number of hairs on our heads. Give Sahara a sense of peace by showing her that her life is not a mistake, but a divine appointment made in the heavens on the day she was born. Father, all children are a precious gift from you, and we praise you for life, health, and strength. I believe you are manipulating the situation in order to gain credit. I pray in Jesus' name. Amen."

CHAPTER EIGHT

Shattered Dreams

FOR THIS FORMER SINGLE MOTHER, having a man take charge and actually be the head of the household is a welcome relief. Although it was difficult for Sahara to give up financial control to Jackson, she has found freedom in the stability of marriage. Sahara is head over heels in love with Jackson, from her hair follicles to her toes. She has never felt such love, such oneness, with anyone as she has with her husband, and within a year, Jackson and Sahara welcomed Adalia, their now nearly one-year-old daughter. Sahara adores not only how much he adores her but also how much he adores their children.

Jackson adores his wife, but his thrill-seeking personality pushes the boundaries of business. Her husband's risky business dealings and unconventional financial decisions have caught up with him, unbeknownst to Sahara.

She is working on a report when she gets a phone call. "Sahara Andrews. How may I assist you?"

"My name is Mary, and I'm calling from First State Bank about the short sale of your rental property, Mrs. Andrews. I have pushed the deadline back to the twentieth."

"I'm sorry, Mary, but I believe you called the wrong account."

Mary examines her file. "Do you and your husband own a three-bedroom, two-bath ranch on Madison Avenue?"

"Yes, we do."

"Then I've got the right account, ma'am. Have a nice day," Mary says as she hangs up the phone.

The phone rings once more.

"Good morning, how may I assist you?" Sahara asks, barely able to concentrate.

"My name is Kenneth Smith. I'm calling from Sunshine Mortgage. Your mortgage is six months past due. How would you like to resolve this situation?"

Sahara, still reeling from the first phone call, manages to ask, "Please excuse me. Could you please repeat that?"

"How would you like to resolve your past-due mortgage payments? This is the final call before we proceed with the foreclosure."

"May I call you back?" Sahara inquires.

"Yes. You have until six p.m. If I don't hear from you, I'll begin the foreclosure process." Kenneth says goodbye and hangs up the phone.

Her phone immediately rang once more.

"Sahara Andrews. How may I assist you?" she says with her heart racing as she anticipates the response.

"Mrs. Andrews, this is an attempt to collect a debt, and this conversation is being recorded. Your payments are three months delinquent, and if a payment arrangement is not made, your vehicle will be repossessed."

Sahara asks, "May I call you back by the end of the day?"

"Yes, we are reachable by telephone until eight p.m."

"Thank you."

Sahara panics as she pulls her phone out of her purse, only to discover she has missed a slew of calls. She sobs while listening to each message, but her sadness quickly turns to rage at Jackson. All of the utility, telecommunications, and insurance providers have left messages about overdue bills.

In order to question Jackson about the couple's finances, Sahara decides to finish up her work early and head home. On the way home, Sahara is reminded of her grandma and dad's voices as they urged her not to marry Jackson.

"What did they see? What did I leave out?" Sahara muses. "How could I have been so naive? What if he has a secret life? What if he has another woman? What will people think? My sisters will be overjoyed with this shocking news! Oh, my daughters! What have I brought into your innocent lives?"

Sahara replays scenes from her life in her mind, looking for clues to who the man she promised to love, cherish, and honor is. At this precise moment, she becomes aware that she has a stranger in her home. Sahara jumps out of the car which is barely in park.

"Jackson! Jackson!" she screams. "Get your black ass down here! Do you hear me, dammit?"

Jackson rushes to answer Sahara's call. "What's the matter with you?" he inquires.

"You've got to be kidding me. I guess you're going to stare me down and act stupid. My problem is bills, bills, unpaid fucking bills! What have you done with our funds? Tell me where my money is."

"Can we discuss this as adults? I'm expecting a World Star cameraman to leap from behind the sofa. I believe you should relax. Then we'll be able to talk," Jackson explains.

"That is the best call and statement I have heard so far today. You're right! I'm too angry to think or speak clearly. Allow me to calm down because I may not be held accountable for my actions,"

Sahara admits as she enters the master bathroom and splashes cold water on her face until it feels numb. She looks at her reflection while patting her face dry.

Jackson goes into their master bedroom and sits in one of the two high-backed wingback chairs with custom upholstery. He talks to himself while he waits for Sahara. "I'm unable to tell her the truth. I need to let her vent, agree with her, and appear very sad."

Sahara stands in the doorway of the bathroom, exhaling deeply. "Please explain. Describe each phone call I received today. Do not, under any circumstances, lie to me!"

Jackson decides to be honest with his wife after noticing her distress. "I love you, and I'm so sorry. Every transaction and decision I made was for the benefit of our family. I work in business. Great risks can sometimes result in large rewards. I can reclaim everything! I guarantee it."

"Get everything back? How much money have you squandered?" As Sahara walks towards her husband, she grills him, "Please respond, dammit! How much?"

Afraid he may lose his wife, Jackson clears his voice. "About one point three million dollars. But, baby, there's another investment opportunity. We're guaranteed to get the money back. I'll have us rolling in dough in no time! You must trust me."

"Hold up. Hold up. Wait a damn minute. We don't have that much money on hand. What did you do? Where did you get that money?" Sahara looks incredulous.

"I took out a line of credit on both houses, I used some of our retirement money, and I used our emergency fund." Jackson has the good sense to look ashamed.

Sahara begins to pace the floor in their master bedroom. "This cannot be happening! I waited. I waited so long to get married. You know what I've been through in my life. How could you betray me?" Sahara begins to weep, and Jackson places both his hands on her shoulders.

"I realize you're upset, and I'm so sorry for keeping this a secret. But give me one more chance, and I promise our big payday is here."

"What is wrong with you? I trusted you! I believed in you! You were supposed to protect me, not feed me to the wolves! We don't have any more money!" exclaims Sahara.

"I was thinking you could ask your dad for a temporary loan. We could pay him back in a year or less."

"When I was single, I didn't ask my dad for money, so I'll be damned if I'm going to ask him for money when I have a man—well, someone who's supposed to be a man. I don't know if you bumped your head or are suffering from a mental break, but what I do know is you need to pack up your belongings and get out!" shouts Sahara, throwing Jackson's clothes into a suitcase she removed from the closet.

"Sweetheart, honey, wait. You're overreacting! Just give me a chance to make it up to you."

"No, I've been through too much. Everyone was right about you. I'm not wasting another minute on you. Now get out!" Sahara insists as she hands Jackson the suitcase.

Taking the suitcase, Jackson retrieves his car keys and shouts, "I love you!" as he leaves their residence.

≈

The following morning, Sahara reviews their financial situation and realizes it is much worse than she had anticipated. She then gets in touch with a lawyer to talk about her options. Sahara displays to Ms. Obu all of her marital transgressions and financial mistreatments during their meeting.

"Sahara, I'm going to suggest that you and your husband file chapter seven bankruptcy first and then move forward with the divorce because of the severity of the debts compared to your annual salary."

"Ms. Obu, I pay my bills. I'm responsible! Is there another possibility?"

"The debts you and your husband have accumulated would take you more than forty years to pay off, not to mention any additional debts he may have related to his businesses. This is the best option for everyone. You'll be able to start over." The attorney paused before continuing, her voice becoming softer this time. "I'm sorry. I realize that this isn't the news you were hoping for."

"No, it's not; but you're the expert. Will I be able to keep my home?"

"No, not if a foreclosure is imminent, unless you file chapter thirteen. You may then be able to save your home, but you may also be required to repay a portion of your debt. This will be determined by the bankruptcy court judge. It is your choice. I can only provide you with my expert opinion."

Sahara exhales. "The chapter seven filing can proceed."

"All right. Maggie, my paralegal, will meet with you to review the paperwork."

Sahara leaves the attorney's office emotionally and spiritually broken.

CHAPTER NINE

Sheep Bites

MILAH IS SLAMMING AND CRAMMING items into a tote as she and Sahara pack their belongings.

Sahara inquires, "Do you wish to discuss it?"

"Why? How I feel is irrelevant to you!" snaps Milah.

"I share your sadness over leaving our home, but we will create new memories in our new residence. We will get through this, sweetheart."

"We were doing well prior to your marriage to Jackson. He's a loser, and because of him, we're losing everything!" Milah screams while running outside.

Sahara has no right to hold her daughter accountable for her behavior. And she is absolutely correct. It was a wonderful life for them, but Jackson has ruined it all. Sahara doesn't stop packing so her daughter can take a breather and collect herself.

Zion has given Sahara, Milah, and Adalia permission to live with him. The upcoming discussion with her half-siblings is something she is dreading.

71

≈

Jazmine greets her dad with a hug and a "good morning" as she enters the house.

"Now that I've seen your stunning face, it's a wonderful morning. Why did you decide to drop by first thing this morning, Jazzy?"

After saying, "I wanted to treat you to breakfast," Jazmine looks around the living room and sees a number of pieces of furniture and boxes lying around in various places. "Where are we at with this? You sure you're not cleaning up for Aunt Z?"

"No. For a while, your sister and her daughters will be staying with me."

"Oh, Daddy, I hope you're not sick."

"You shouldn't be concerned. My health is excellent. There's a rough patch in your sister and her family's life. She is in need of our love and prayers."

"I assume that another of her bad decisions has come back to haunt her, and her innocent daughters have been caught in the crossfire. When is she going to grow up?"

"Jazzy, don't be like that. Whatever decisions she makes, she is still your sister. It's her choice, and it's her life. To be honest, we're all one decision away from disaster. This does not imply that she is a bad person or a bad mother."

"You'll always see the best in her."

"I see the best in every one of my children. I adore you all, flaws and all," Zion admits.

"This is our childhood home, where we have fond memories of our mother and our family. Sahara has infiltrated every aspect of our lives. What will she take next from us?"

Zion takes a step forward and faces his daughter. "Nobody can ever take away what we shared as a family. I'd do the same thing for any of you that I'm doing for Sahara. I totally love you all and wish you the best. Some things in life are beyond our control, and hindsight is always twenty-twenty. Sahara is going through enough without her family passing judgment on her," Zion expresses sympathy.

"When will they arrive?"

"When Sahara gets home from work. Mother Spencer will be over later to assist them in settling in."

"Okay, Daddy. I'm going to the shop. I'm no longer hungry. Have a wonderful day! I love you."

"I love you even more, Jazzy," Zion says as his daughter walks out the door.

≈

Jazmine is so enraged that she has to talk to Corrin on the phone.

"Hello," answers Corrin. "What's up, sis?"

"Girl, you will not believe the foolery that's fallen into Daddy's lap."

"From what exactly has Dad rescued Sahara?" Corrin asks sarcastically.

"I have no idea what happened between her and her husband, but Dad is moving her and the girls into his house today!" Jazmine shouts.

"What? Are you serious? That's the only part of our lives she hasn't tainted with her dysfunction. She's taken our mother, father, and now our childhood home. This is far too much!"

"You know Daddy is all protective. Nothing you say or do will persuade him to change his mind. Sahara is his beloved mirror image and the youngest."

"We'll see about that!" exclaims Corrin as she slams the phone down, ending her conversation with Jazmine.

≈

"Aren't you a pleasant sight? Come on in and let me assist you with your bags," Mother Spencer says as Sahara and Milah enter Zion's home, the baby in Sahara's arms.

"Mom-Mom, I got it. I can't have you out here yanking on these bags. Take Adalia for me. Where is Daddy?"

"Your father is finishing up at work. He'll be here shortly. I'm as tough as an ox when it comes to these bags. Don't be fooled by my age."

"Mom-Mom, you'll never change," Sahara says before handing the baby to her grandmother.

"Milah, please go upstairs. I've set you up in Dexter's old room. I hope you like the modifications I made for you," Mother Spencer says. Milah walks upstairs with a half-smile on her face.

Mother Spencer and Sahara are sitting on the comfortable, deep-seat sofa with plush cushions in the family room.

"How are you holding up?"

"I'm not sure how long I can keep up this brave act," Sahara admits. "I'm heartbroken. Who would have guessed that after all these years of battling, succeeding, and living the American dream, I'd be moving into my father's house as an adult? I can't say I blame my daughter for looking at me with contempt in her eyes. I brought this man into our lives, and he's completely destroyed it. You and my father were correct. What's the matter with me? Why do I keep making such poor choices in men?" Sahara starts crying uncontrollably.

"Listen carefully, Sahara. We all make mistakes, and learning is an important part of life. Some things are more difficult to learn than others. You made a decision about a man before you had all of the facts. Everything positive about him was emphasized. He did not disclose his proclivity for gambling, risky investments, or whatever you want to call it, and neither did anyone in his family. All of these get-rich-quick schemes are risky. What you didn't realize hurt you. It is not your fault! I can only imagine how deeply this betrayal stings. But you have family, and we care about you. We'll help you and the girls get through this difficult time. Thank goodness Adalia is too young to understand what's going on," Mother Spencer says as she holds Sahara's hand.

Zion walks into the family room. "I'm here, baby girl."

"Daddy!" Sahara says softly. As she stands, her father grips her tightly.

"Everything will be fine. I've got you."

"It hurts so bad, Daddy. It hurts. It hurts," Sahara sobs, her face pressed against her father's chest.

"I know, baby." Mother Spencer and Zion are moved to tears as they witness Sahara's agony.

"Come with me, Sahara," Zion says as he takes his daughter's hand in his. They make their way upstairs, Mother Spencer close behind. "I've got a surprise for you. Nothing beats your own personal space. I understand you'll only be here for a short time, but I wanted you to be as comfortable as possible." Zion walks into her newly remodeled master bedroom.

"Daddy, it's beautiful. I can't accept this. It's too much."

"You can and will. Nothing is ever enough for my girls. This was dubbed 'serene glamour' by the designer, whatever that means. Mom assisted in the design."

"Do you like it, Sahara?" Mother Spencer inquires.

"Like it? Love it! The fabrics are lovely in gray and light purple. Over my bed, there is a bubble and crystal chandelier. The gold mirror and shaggy pillows push this room over the top. You two went above and beyond. I'm incredibly grateful to have you in my life. Thank you so much. One day I'll try to make you proud of me," says Sahara.

"You already have my admiration. At such a young age, you've accomplished so much. You have endured. Never give that up or let anyone take it from you." Zion pauses before embracing Sahara once more. "I'll take the rest of your possessions from your car."

"Take some time for yourself," Mother Spencer advises. "I will make sure Milah is comfortable in her space. The bathroom is stocked with fresh towels and a change of pajamas. In roughly an hour, we will have dinner ready. Dear, we genuinely love you."

"I'm blown away and so thankful. Thank you," Sahara says as Zion and Mother Spencer leave the huge master bedroom suite and shut the door behind them.

Sahara has always been proud of the fact that she has been able to get out of trouble on her own. This time is not the same. She feels like every bad choice she's made is pulling her down. It's as if a wave of despair as deep as an ocean is pulling her down. "I have to battle. I can do better," Sahara says to herself as she fills the big clawfoot tub with lavender bubble bath. As she goes deeper into the foamy, lava-like liquid, every muscle in her body hurts and feels tense. Sahara says to herself, "Mm, I needed this," as she rests her head on the bath pillow.

When she hears a knock on the door, she jumps.

"Yes?"

"Honey, it's almost time for dinner. Are you joining us?" Mother Spencer asks.

"Yes, ma'am. I'll be down there in a few minutes." Sahara looks at the clock on the wall and says, "What time is it?" Her unplanned nap lasted nearly an hour. The water in her tub has gotten cold, so she rushes to finish taking a bath.

Her body moisturized and clad in pajamas and slippers, Sahara walks downstairs, the aroma of pure deliciousness infiltrating her nostrils. "Mom-Mom, you're spoiling us. I don't cook like this. What's for dinner?" asks Sahara.

Creamed cornbread, chicken and dumplings, sautéed peas, and peach pound cake for dessert," Mother Spencer grins.

"While you were being a slowpoke, I'm having my second bowl. Milah, Adalia, and I have been getting it in. Aren't we, beautiful? She can eat, too," says Zion.

"I know she can because she's greedy," Sahara jokes.

The family is having a good ole time, sharing memories and eating great food. Zion has even been able to make Milah laugh, which gives Sahara a glimmer of hope. Suddenly there's a knock on the door along with the doorbell chiming throughout the prodigious home.

"I'll get it. Were you expecting anyone?" asks Zion.

"No, sir. I hope it's not Jackson. I don't want to see him," responds Sahara.

Zion opens the door and Corrin glares at her father with fire in her eyes. "Good evening, Father, may I come in?"

"Of course. We were just having dinner. Have you eaten?" inquires Zion.

"Yes, I have, but thank you. Good evening, everyone," Corrin says as she enters. Her family members respond in unison. "The house looks nice. Have you been remodeling?" Corrin investigates.

"Change and upgrades are good. I like it very much. Thanks for noticing. The designer and I didn't do as much downstairs as we did upstairs. That's where the real transformation took place," admits Zion.

Mother Spencer can tell that Corrin's spirit has changed, so she asks, "Corrin, why don't you sit down and tell us about how busy you are? I hear from all along the coast about the great things you do in the community and in ministry."

"I'd be glad to talk about that. Can you show me around upstairs, Sahara? I'd love to see the beautiful changes that my dad has made to the house where I grew up," Corrin says, her voice sounding harsh.

Mother Spencer says, "I can show you."

"I'm fine. I'll show her," Sahara says as she gets up from the table. The two sisters proceed upstairs.

"Do you think that was a wise decision?" Mother Spencer inquires of Zion.

"Momma, Sahara is capable of handling herself."

≈

"Milah is happy to show you around her room. This is the room that Daddy designed for me."

"Wow, it's beautiful," Corrin exclaims. "I had no idea my father ran a homeless shelter. You've reached a new low. How dare you come into our home and desecrate my, Jazz's, and Dex's most sacred spaces? Is there nothing else you can take from us?" Corrin is fuming.

"I'm sick and tired of being used as a scapegoat for your illogical conspiracy theories," Sahara retorts. "My life is not centered on you. I don't intentionally hurt people. You stand on platforms proclaiming God's love and your status as a sheep in His pasture. Sheep, according to my research, do not bite! Why don't you stop preaching to me and start doing what you preach?" Sahara exclaims before turning around and leaving Corrin standing in the middle of the bedroom.

CHAPTER TEN

Ungodly Alliance

CORRIN IS STILL IRRITATED BY Zion bailing Sahara out of her problems, even though Jazmine is preoccupied with the day-to-day operations of her businesses. Dexter is unconcerned about his sisters' criticism of Sahara or her choices, and Corrin should forget about contacting her father or Mother Spencer. She calls Auntie Z because she has no one else to vent her vile rage on.

"Good morning, Corrin. What am I to thank for this wonderful surprise?"

"I'm not sure I'm going to be pleasant today."

"What's the matter, my dear? Is there a problem?"

"I'm afraid I'll come across as petty, and I feel childish. Perhaps I'm confused and unable to process how I feel. Grrr, this is so annoying."

"Let us discuss it. I'd like to be there for you. You may address me as if I were your mother."

"Auntie Z, I appreciate it. My mother appears to be the only person who comprehends my situation. My father loves me, but when

79

it comes to Sahara, he has blinders on. She possesses everything! Amazing daughters, a career, a husband who goes out of his way to please her, but most importantly, Father's unwavering love and support. He's renovated my childhood home to make room for her and her daughters. She's nearly taken over his house! My mother would roll over in her grave if she saw the house she built destroyed by that cretin!"

"I can only imagine how difficult it must be to be a bystander while your childhood home is being demolished. You have many happy memories of your mother and father in that house. These are the things you can keep and cherish. I have a feeling Champagne would advise you to do just that," Zena declares.

"My mother should be in that house right now! I constantly think about her. How different my life would be if she hadn't been taken away from me. Sahara is prancing around Father's house like a queen bee. Whatever Sahara desires, Father and Mother Spencer will go out of their way to make it happen. I'm sick of it!"

"Do you and your siblings feel neglected by Zion?"

"No way, no how. Father adores us and supports us in all of our endeavors. He has never missed a significant event in our lives. However, there is an unspoken truth: Sahara unmistakably resembles Father, and the shooting, as well as his undying lust for her homewrecking mother, make her his favorite. I can tell by the way he looks at her and how his voice changes when he talks about her. He and Sahara have a bond that he does not have with the rest of us," Corrin admits.

"Bonds can be severed. Champagne was concerned that Zion's infidelity would have a negative impact on her children. Sahara was conceived through infidelity. She can't stop the evil she creates because her conception was evil. We'll reveal Sahara for who she is, and we'll be there to help Zion pick up the pieces of his broken heart," Zena exclaims.

"Thank goodness I have someone on my side who believes in me. I don't want my father to be exploited, and I can see Sahara riding off into the sunset with our inheritance," Corrin confirms.

"I really like you and apologize for not being there for you sooner. Nothing can keep me away now, and we'll expose the truth about Sahara and shame the devil together!" Zena asserts.

CHAPTER ELEVEN

Pain on Steroids

S AHARA RETURNS TO WORK AFTER a brief hiatus to reconsider her life's path. This financial saga with Jackson is embarrassing to say the least, but Sahara enters her workplace eager to get back to work. It has remained her only constant throughout her life. Her coworkers enthusiastically greet her.

"We've really missed you, girl. It felt like months, not a couple of weeks. Your boss is a demanding and arrogant jerk. How can you stand the way he speaks to you?" Cara inquires.

"I ignore him."

"He believes he is the greatest thing since sliced bread. I have sympathy for his wife. I can only imagine what he does to her."

Sahara laughs. "Where has everyone gone? When I returned, I expected to face a mountain of work."

"I have no idea. The top brass have been meeting since first thing this morning. I don't care what they do as long as they stay out of my hair," Cara responds.

"Tell me how you really feel, Cara," Sahara jokes. With that, the two ladies proceed to their desks and begin working.

Then Sahara's phone beeps and a voice from the speaker asks, "Good morning, Sahara, can you join us in the conference room?"

"Yes, sir. I'll be there shortly."

"What in the world is that about?" Cara inquires.

"Who knows what these privileged jerks are capable of. Perhaps someone forgot to put the avocado on their sandwich," Sahara responds, and the ladies laugh as she walks out of the office.

She takes the elevator to the fifth floor where she can see, through the soundproof glass walls, the company's executive director, human resources manager, and Sahara's immediate supervisor. They're all seated around the conference table.

"Good morning, Sahara," Dave, her boss, says.

"Good day, everyone. What exactly is going on?"

"Please find a seat. We need to talk about something with you," Mr. Craven, the executive director, instructs.

"Sahara, we're meeting with you today to discuss our concerns about a matter that was brought to our attention anonymously," Dave says. "I received a package in the mail last week that contained a copy of your and your husband's bankruptcy filing. We pride ourselves and stake our reputation on having qualified, responsible financial team leaders as the face of our brand at Synergy Financial. You have direct access to many of our high-profile clients. Can you comment on the authenticity of these documents?"

Sahara lets out a breath. "Yes, my husband and I are declaring bankruptcy before our divorce. I'm not sure how this affects my job performance."

"Our entire brand, Sahara, is built on fiscal responsibility, accountability, and becoming debt-free and financially independent," Mr. Craven says. "We believe that bankruptcy absolves the consumer's obligation to pay their debts. That contradicts our core philosophy.

With that said, we must regretfully terminate your employment with us, effective immediately."

"We will include an additional fifteen hundred dollars in your final paycheck due to your current circumstances. This isn't about you, Sahara. We think you're a wonderful person, but we need to protect our brand's reputation. Best wishes for your future endeavors," Dave says solemnly.

Sahara is unable to muster a single word in defense, and the men rise and leave the conference room. Sahara is completely taken aback and sits alone in the minimalist, modern conference room, her thoughts racing as she wonders how she will begin to rebuild her new life without work. When Sahara is finally able to return to her office, she takes a box from the closet and begins to clear her desk. The sounds of pens hitting picture frames and folders being thrown into a box pique the interest of Sahara's coworker.

"What the Sam Hell is going on in here?" Cara inquires.

"Don't make this any more difficult for me. They fired me! When it rains, it pours," Sahara says as she continues to slam items into the box.

"Friend, no. What will I do if I don't have you? Now I'm the only black person up here again. I'm going to miss you a lot. You should keep in touch," Cara says to Sahara as she hugs her and has tears in her eyes.

"Don't do this to me. You can't break me down. I've kept it together. Girl, I have to walk out of here with my head held high. Dry your eyes. I'll be fine. I always am. We'll stay in touch," Sahara reassures her, lifting the box filled with the remnants of what used to be her office.

Cara opens the door for her, and Dave enters unexpectedly, asking, "Can I have a minute?"

"One," Sahara says. Cara closes the door and returns to her desk.

"I'm sorry this has happened to you, Sahara. I wish you'd come to me instead. When the corporate office got those papers, I couldn't do anything about it," explains Dave.

"Communication must be two-way. You could have approached me with your concerns. For many years, I have successfully represented this company and my clients. This isn't right, but the Lord gives and takes. Thank you for the lesson and the chance. Have a wonderful day!" As Sahara lifts her box, Dave opens the door for her.

Employees gasp and shake their heads, while others turn away from their workstations. Her departure from Synergy Financial is confirmed by the sunlight shining through the glass door. Once outside, the gravity of her dismissal from her longtime employer, bankruptcy, and the dissolution of her marriage causes her to collapse. She opens her vehicle's liftgate with her foot and throws the box into the trunk. Sahara is sobbing by the time she gets behind the wheel and drives away from the employee parking lot for the last time.

CHAPTER TWELVE

Just Sleep

FTER A FEW WEEKS, SAHARA believes Jackson has ruined everything good in her life. Her credit is ruined, she's lost her home and had to auction off her few remaining assets to pay bill collectors, and now her one constant source of comfort is gone.

When Sahara's sisters decide to pay her and Milah a visit at their father's house, they find Sahara lying across the sofa in the family room, a box of tissues beside her. This stunning vixen's shoulder-length, passion-plum hair is pulled up into a messy bun. Her eyes are puffy, and she has a stuffy nose from crying. She hasn't bathed in days. A long, dark-blue bathrobe conceals her body odor and covers her five-foot-nine, hourglass frame. Her outfit is completed by a pair of fuzzy socks. Milah hasn't returned home from school yet, and Corrin and Jazmine have entered their family's home.

"Oh, my dear, what seems to have gotten you so down?" Corrin asks from behind.

Too upset to participate in this toxic banter, Sahara responds, "I'm going to be fine. Thanks."

"You can't sit here all day crying about your problems. You are not the first or the last woman to be betrayed by a man. You have children and should get your act together!" Jazmine snaps her fingers.

"Have you even tried to find a new job, or do you intend to live off Daddy's money?" Corrin conducts an investigation.

"Is this the modern role of ministers, to figuratively kick people when they're down? I'm at a loss for words right now and can't really contribute anything to the conversation. I'm just hanging out here, not bothering anyone. Are you here to gloat or something?"

"Well, you do have a history of making poor choices," Corrin says with a malicious tone. "When I believe you have reached your lowest point, you prove me wrong. Honestly, I feel terrible for your daughters. They deserve a much better mother than you. These innocent children have endured incalculable trauma throughout their brief lives. For their sake, I would expect you to do better and improve. However, I would then be the one expecting too much from a mistake."

Sahara rises from the couch and enters the kitchen. She removes a bowl from the cabinet, retrieves ice cream from the freezer, and scoops some into the bowl.

"Funny. You can locate the refrigerator but cannot locate a job. Pathetic!" snaps Jazmine.

"I've had enough of being your verbal punching bag! I used to feel sorry for you, but now I understand why Daddy loved my mother. She's sweet, compassionate, loving, forgiving, and rational, and she sacrificed her own happiness to ensure you grew up in the same house as him. You try to make fun of me in order to feel superior. Everyone knows that if my mother had said the word, Daddy would have dropped everything to be with us. No matter how many accolades you receive, how much money you make, or how many people applaud your phony asses, you'll always be what Daddy settled for because he couldn't have the life he truly desired. So, why are you fuckwits here?" Corrin and Jazmine stand there, stunned, astonished by Sahara's newly discovered spine.

"Why are we here?" Jazmine asks.

"That's a good question," Mother Spencer says as she walks into the kitchen, setting her grocery bags on the kitchen counter.

"We've come to bring you gifts for your daughter. Milah's birthday is today," Corrin declares.

Corrin's announcement of Milah's birthday shocks Sahara and snaps her out of her depressive trance.

"Child, you forgot your own daughter's birthday," Jazmine quips, shaking her head sarcastically.

"I told Milah you weren't feeling well but wanted to get her something for her special day," Mother Spencer explains.

Corrin and Jazmin roll their eyes as they realize Mother Spencer has come to Sahara's aid once more.

"Why don't you girls do something useful and assist an old lady? On the back seat of my car, there's a cake, a large teddy bear, balloons, and a card. Could you please bring them in for me?" Mother Spencer inquires.

"Yes, ma'am," Corrin and Jazmine respond, retrieving a cake beautifully decorated with pink, purple, and white flowers.

"Are you staying for ice cream and cake with us, girls? Milah and a few of her friends will arrive within the hour." Mother Spencer says.

"No way, ma'am. We'll leave Milah's gifts on the coffee table," Corrin responds.

"Okay, kids. Give me some sugar before you go about your business," Mother Spencer says as she hugs Corrin and Jazmine goodbye.

Sahara is sitting at the island, eating her ice cream, when Mother Spencer enters the kitchen to put away the items she purchased.

"Thank you so much, Mom-Mom. I can't believe I forgot my daughter's birthday. My sisters are right. I'm a loser. Milah would be better off without me."

"You're talking nonsense now. Life can teach us difficult lessons. I'm not aware of anyone who marries in order to divorce. You love deeply and easily forgive. That can be both a blessing and a curse. Healthy boundaries must be established in all relationships, not just romantic relationships. You teach people how to treat you. Jackson has a good heart, but he's a risk taker. He's not stable, and you need a man who can be relied on."

"Grandma, I'm shattered. I'm dying on the inside. The agony is unbearable. I don't want to be in pain any longer. I just want to sleep without waking up. My siblings all have their own lives. My life makes me feel embarrassed. I can't bear looking in the mirror. Milah despises me. She is correct in blaming me for our loss. It's all my fault! I chose to be with this man, which turned out to be the biggest mistake of my life." Sahara starts crying.

"You'll make it, and you'll be rewarded twice as much. You're a good person, a wonderful mother, and a wonderful wife. You just attempted to put a crown on a clown, which never works." Mother Spencer and Sahara burst out laughing as she says this. "I heard the young folks say that." Mother Spencer continues to smile.

"Pay attention, baby. The Lord works in mysterious ways, and we never know what awaits us in life. I want you to go upstairs, take a hot shower, get dressed, put on some makeup, and be ready for Milah and her friends when they arrive. She deserves to feel special today."

Sahara nods and follows her grandmother's instructions.

Mother Spencer hangs party decorations and places balloons throughout the living room and kitchen while Sahara is upstairs. She's about to finish when Milah and three of her friends walk in.

"Where's the birthday girl?" exclaims Sahara as she opens her arms to embrace Milah.

"Don't embarrass me, Mom," Milah says shyly.

"You mean like this?" Sahara teases, kissing Milah on the cheeks. Her friends greeted with laughter Sahara and Mother Spencer.

"Don't laugh because you can get some of these kisses as well," Sahara says, smiling.

"Thank you very much, Momma."

Milah is smiling, giggling, and talking loudly with her friends about the food, decorations, and cake, and everyone has a good time until the parents of Milah's friends arrive to pick up their children. Milah is now in her room, on the phone with her friends and admiring her gifts. Mother Spencer and Sahara clean until there is no trace of the party. Sahara goes to the bathroom to remove her makeup while Mother Spencer retreats to her in-law suite to rest her aching joints.

She wraps a silk scarf around her head, and dresses in warm fleece pajamas. Then Sahara looks in the mirror at herself, and tears begin to flow from her eyes.

"You're right. Milah despises you! She'd be better off with your sister, Corrin. You forgot her birthday. Except for you, everyone else was able to buy her a gift. Her very own mother! Your family is always expected to bail you out. Aren't you sick of them rescuing you? You're a failure and a disaster! They must rescue you from yourself. Why don't you relieve them of that burden? Sahara, if you want to sleep, just sleep. There's a bottle of muscle relaxants here; take the whole thing. Then you'll be able to rest and the pain will be gone. Do it!" implores the suicide spirit.

Sahara picks up the bottle, unscrews the cap, and empties it into her mouth, swallowing all of the pills.

"You're mine now!" exclaims the spirit of suicide.

Memories of her daughter, father, and Mother Spencer flash through Sahara's mind. She realizes she's made a mistake and starts to vomit the pills down the toilet.

"You're a failure. You can't even kill yourself," says the spirit of suicide.

Sahara examines herself in the mirror as she rinses the pill residue from her mouth. "I could be a failure. I may not be as smart as my siblings or have as much money as they do, but I refuse to give up! God, please help me not to give up!" Sahara declares.

Sahara, now afraid of falling asleep, retreats downstairs to the family room to watch television. A knock on the front door followed by the sound of keys alerts her. God knows she's not looking forward to seeing her sisters again. "Hello, sis. I felt the need to check in on you. I also have some money and a card for Milah."

Dex leans over and hugs Sahara, who is sitting on the couch, before taking a seat beside her. "I absolutely love you, bro. It's been a rough day, if not a rough couple of months."

"Jazzy told me she and Corrin had a run-in with you today. Question. Fuckwits; really. Where did that come from, valley girl?" Dex teasingly asks.

"Listen, I'm going through too much right now to even have a conversation with them. It's emotionally draining, and I'm over it. We are related by blood, but how you treat me is what makes us family. I will love them from afar. They are far too toxic," declares Sahara.

"Even though it's Milah's birthday, I have something for you as well." Dex takes a medical marijuana vamp pen from his jacket pocket. "Are you trying to get Mother Spencer in here pleading the blood of Jesus?"

"It has no odor, sis." Dex smiles sheepishly as he takes a drag from the vape and hands it to Sahara. She takes a drag. They both start giggling at each other. "And when are you going to settle down? I'd like to have some nieces and nephews before I'm too old to play with them."

"Hey, this is your cheering-up session. There will be no discussion of my personal life. You're not going to have me around here crying and singing Lenny Williams' Because I Love You. Hell naw! It will happen when it is supposed to happen. I want a woman to love me for who I am and not for how much money I have."

"You are a good, hardworking, caring man who will make an excellent father and husband."

"Whatever you say, sis. But, are you really good?"

"No, but I will be. I have no other option but to push past how I feel until I don't feel this way anymore."

"I know you're a very proud woman. You are not a charity cause; you are my baby sister. I know you wouldn't take money from me if I put it in your hands. So, I wired five thousand dollars to your account today. Do something nice for yourself or with the girls. Get your mojo back! Reconnect with yourself. You can reclaim what you lost," Dex says as he looks Sahara in the eyes.

Sahara's eyes fill with tears. "Thank you for always being there for me. I love you to the moon and back," Sahara says as she hugs her brother once more.

He then snatches the vamp pen from her grasp. "That's enough mushy stuff. You're tinkering with it. Check out what's playing on Netflix," Dex says as the two laugh hysterically throughout the evening while watching Dave Chappelle stand-up.

CHAPTER THIRTEEN

Strength in Weakness

THE NEXT MORNING, SAHARA AWAKENS with a profound new lease on life. Scrapple, sliced ham, scrambled eggs, grits, fruit, orange juice, and coffee greet her children, Zion, and Mother Spencer.

"Good morning, Momma," Milah says as she walks into the kitchen, Adalia in her arms. Zion and Mother Spencer trail close behind.

"To God be the glory for this delicious meal. You're up early, getting your Betty Crocker on," Mother Spencer snickers as she teases her.

"I'm delighted to see you up so early. You haven't seen me off to school in a long time, and breakfast is delicious. Momma, I've missed your cooking," Milah explains.

"I know, baby. I'm sorry Mommy hasn't been herself for a while, but I'm much better now. Things are going to improve for us. I promise," Sahara declares as she kisses Milah on the cheek.

Zion watches Sahara as she serves everyone breakfast and admires her fortitude. He takes a sip of his coffee before asking, "What's your plan, baby girl?"

After breakfast, Milah joins Mother Spencer in taking Adalia upstairs to freshen up for daycare.

Sahara inhales deeply.

"I never want to feel like anyone or an employer has this much power over my ability to care for my children, Daddy. It's taken me years to build myself up from nothing, despite my bad decisions, and I'm exhausted! My entire existence feels like a struggle. I'm tired of fighting for everything in my life: a fight to stay alive, a fight to keep a roof over my head, a fight to keep a job, a fight to keep a man!"

"Sahara, I've never been prouder of you than I am right now. There is no shame in suffering. It's much easier to give up than it is to keep fighting. You may feel weak, but you have always possessed tremendous inner strength. You're at your best right now," says Zion, looking into his daughter's eyes.

"I'm not feeling particularly strong. I've failed at so many things over the years. My marriage was the one thing I was certain of, and it, like everything else, failed. What kind of mother would be so blinded by love that I missed Jackson's instability that you and Mom-Mom saw? You were correct. How come I couldn't see it?"

"We were on the outside looking in…and you don't get to be this old and still be a fool. Game recognizes game," Zion responds slyly. "Do you have a plan?"

"Yes, I do. How did you come to that conclusion?"

"You have the same look in your eyes that your mother used to get when she set her mind to something. So, how can I help?"

"Here's what I'm considering. By being their best brand ambassador and building relationships with their high-dollar clients, I helped my previous employer make millions of dollars. Because of my bankruptcy, I'll probably have a difficult time finding comparable work, but I'm a Spencer. Why should I look for opportunities when I can create my own? Daddy, I'd like to start my own marketing company called Say My Name. What are your thoughts?"

"I think it's a fantastic idea, and the name is incredibly catchy! I've always suspected you had the potential to be an entrepreneur. I saw how hard you worked to close deals, and you never asked me for anything. I understand you're a very proud young lady, and accepting my invitation to live here was difficult for you. Please allow me to assist you on your entrepreneurial journey."

"Okay, Daddy. Thank you for always being there for me. We're going to do this together!" exclaims Sahara.

"I love you and will always want the best for you, my sweet girl!" The two get up from the table and hug each other tightly until the sound of a horn honking interrupts them.

Milah dashes down the stairs, out the door, to catch her bus. "Bye," she exclaims. "I love you!"

"Love you more!" exclaim Sahara and Zion together.

Adalia and Mother Spencer return, dressed and ready to ride out. "I can drop Little Miss off at daycare today, Sahara. Will you be able to get her?" Mother Spencer inquires.

"Yes, ma'am, and thank you so much for everything you've done for us. I appreciate it."

"You're more than welcome, baby. After that, I'm going to the senior center to beat Mother Pearl in bingo."

Sahara kisses Adalia goodbye, and Zion assists his mother in carrying his granddaughter and her baby bag to the car before watching them drive away. Sahara is finishing cleaning the kitchen when he returns inside. Zion is overjoyed that she is relying on him and sharing her dreams with him.

"Would you like a helping hand?"

Sahara gives her father a friendly smile. "Yes, please. Thank you."

"There's nothing to thank me for. I'm your father. There's nowhere I'd rather be than by your side."

Sahara rests her head on her father's shoulder for a moment. He then begins to tell her stories about Mother Spencer making him clean baseboards and windowsills as a child, as well as the rest of her cleaning rituals. They laugh so hard that tears well up in their eyes.

CHAPTER FOURTEEN

Exhale

SAHARA IS BECOMING A BETTER version of herself every day. She's been up extra early every morning, as she promised Milah, preparing nutritious breakfasts and packing her and Adalia's lunches.

Zion contacted one of his longtime colleagues, Jules Fuentes, a marketing juggernaut. "Hello there, my friend. We haven't spoken in a long time. How is the family doing?"

"We're fantastic! All of the children have graduated from college. Thank God for that, because college is so expensive these days. I made the decision to go semi-retired," Mr. Fuentes responds.

"I'm glad to hear you might have some free time because I have a project that could benefit from your stellar expertise. Are you interested in being a mentor?" Zion inquires.

"Sure, for the right person. Some of the new cats in the game want all of the rewards but lack the work ethic. I am not a babysitter, and I will not spoon-feed adults. Who are you thinking of?"

"Sahara is my youngest daughter. She's a smart, hard worker who needs Yoda's advice to get her company off to a good start. I'm confident you can give her what I can't. Marketing isn't my strong suit, and I know when to stick to my strengths."

"I recall her. She's the one who kept going to school while pregnant, right?"

"Yes."

"I like her. She's tough. I'd be honored to assist her, but I will not be gentle with her because she's your daughter," Mr. Fuentes asserts emphatically.

"I would never request preferential treatment. I doubt Sahara would want that. She's stronger than she appears."

"That's fantastic! You're presenting an old man with a new challenge. Please have her meet me at my office on Monday at ten a.m.," Mr. Fuentes explains.

"I owe you and thank you!"

"No worries. Over the years, you've helped me make a lot of money. It will also keep an old man from getting in trouble with his wife.

"No worries. You have contributed to my wealth over the years. In addition, it will keep me out of trouble with my wife."

Before ending their call, the gentlemen exchange pleasantries. Zion cannot wait to tell Sahara the good news when he next sees her.

While the children are at school, Sahara invests in herself by reading, conducting research, taking online courses, and attending marketing seminars. Even to complete her business plan, she uses an online platform.

The children enter the house first, followed by a sluggish Sahara.

Adalia yells, "Hi, Pop-Pop!" as she approaches Zion to give him a high five.

"Hello, precious. How's Pop-Pop's little peanut?"

"I'm not a nut. I'm a girl," the precocious preschooler exclaims.

Zion chuckles as Milah embraces and kisses him on the cheek.

"Hi, Pop-Pop! I will take Little Miss Grownie upstairs."

"Adalia cannot help herself. She already has the Spencer mouth. You girls get ready for dinner," Zion remarks, observing how visibly weary Sahara appears. He tells her, "Tonight, I will prepare dinner so you can relax. Why don't you get settled like your daughters? Allow Daddy to care for my daughters."

Sahara embraces her father and murmurs, "Thank you!"

Zion orders food from Indulge, a local upscale soul food restaurant with delicious pastries. He orders jerk chicken, fried chicken with honey-pepper sauce, chicken tenders for Adalia, macaroni and cheese, collard greens with smoked turkey wings, yams, salad, and the restaurant's renowned buttered-rum pound cake. As his daughter and grandchildren walk downstairs, Zion is tipping the delivery driver. He places the food bags on the dining table and empties them.

"Milah, could you grab a few plates and utensils from the cabinet?"

"Yes, sir."

"I knew you wouldn't be cooking, but I was expecting pizza. You went all out as if we're celebrating a special event," Sahara ruminates over the containers of appetizing food.

"I never need an excuse to spoil my girls. You have worked to prepare for the launch of your business. I desired to do something thoughtful for you. In addition, I have some good news for you."

"It must be excellent. You are grinning like a Cheshire cat," Sahara suggests as she prepares Adalia's meal.

As everyone is enjoying dinner, Zion asks Sahara, "How would you feel about being mentored by one of the best in the industry?"

Sahara chokes on her coke. She exclaims, while swallowing hard, "Yes! Who? How?"

"One of my friends used to be a partner at one of the largest mid-Atlantic marketing firms. He has worked in the industry for over thirty years. I spoke with him today, and he agreed to be your mentor. Jules Fuentes is his name. You'll meet him at ten a.m. on Monday. I'll email you his contact information—don't be late. He despises tardiness because time is money to him. Jules believes that wasting time means wasting money. He has zero tolerance for either. He is on time if he arrives fifteen minutes early. In his eyes, arriving on time is late. Please take advantage of this fantastic opportunity. Be ready to learn. He's direct and will test you to see what you're made of. I am so proud of you and know you will succeed. I have faith in you."

Sahara's eyes well up with tears. "I won't fail you, Daddy. You've done so much for my family and me. I'm not sure how I'll ever repay you. I am grateful to have you in my life and don't take it for granted."

"If you fail, pick yourself up and try again. This time is different. I can sense it! You're going to accomplish incredible things. Succeeding is sufficient recompense. You're my heart, and I still regret missing so much of your life. I feel like I'll never be able to make up for the time I lost with you," proclaims Zion.

"Let it all go, Daddy. You couldn't help what you didn't know, and I had a wonderful life. You're the best father a girl could ask for. I hope my daughters have husbands who are as devoted to them as you are to me. The rest is ancient history. Right now, we're all here together. That is most important to me. We're healthy, safe, and heading in the right direction. I haven't been this happy in a long time, and it's all because of you, Daddy."

"I played a minor role in assisting you. You overcame loss and depression and continue to astound me with your inner strength," Zion says as he rubs his daughter's hand.

Milah smiles as she watches her mother and grandfather interact. In her eyes, her pop-pop is a superhero who helped her mother rediscover her love of life.

CHAPTER FIFTEEN

Excuses

SAHARA RUSHES TO GET ADALIA to daycare after Milah boards the bus. She spent the entire weekend preparing for her meeting with Jules Fuentes.

Sahara goes to her favorite coffee shop, Black Out, which is only a few minutes away from her appointment. She orders her coffee and takes a seat at a table while she waits.

A familiar voice says, "Good morning, lovely. I've been missing you and the kids. Can I have a few minutes of your time?" Jackson inquires.

"I've got an appointment. Make it happen quick."

"I'm collaborating with a few other investors on a new project, darling. I am trying. This may be the big break we've been waiting for and it can help bring our family back together."

"Are you insane, Negro? I lost everything because of your decisions, which also affect our children. It displaced them and rendered us homeless. We lost the house where they grew up. So, why would I want to go backward? I was proud of myself for building a life without the help of my parents, but you forced me to turn to them. I had no choice but to accept my father's help. I felt inadequate. You made me look foolish. Now I'm pulling myself together by God's grace, and all you can say is that you're trying. If I tried as hard as you did, we'd be sleeping in a cardboard box under a bridge. If a child attempted to walk for as long as you have tried, the parent would have it evaluated for a developmental delay! When are you going to stop trying and start doing?" Sahara inhaled and exhaled deeply.

"Never mind," she continues, "this is a senseless conversation. In a month, our divorce will be final. I'll agree to Adalia having biweekly visitation. We have nothing else to talk about. I'm not convinced! I don't believe you! I'm not interested in you! We will co-parent, but we are nothing more. Stop attempting to get me back. I am gone! The love is no longer there. You have betrayed me to the point I can hardly bear to look at you. I forgive you, but I'm over this marriage disaster. I am deserving of better. I expect more. I want more and my children and I will be better off without you and your instability in the household. You are too unstable. When you're ready to begin visitation with Adalia, please text me. Keep in mind that you did this to us!" Sahara insists, then stands after hearing her name called by the barista.

"Wait!" yells Jackson as he grabs Sahara's arm. Sahara glares at him, and he lets go of his grip. "Please, this cannot be the end. Tell me what I need to do. I'll do anything to make this right. You know I've never loved anyone as much as I love you. You're my best friend and the only person who has ever believed in me. I can't afford to lose you! You know that I grew up with an angry father and a passive mother. We can go to counseling or whatever you want!" Jackson begs.

"The problem is, I don't want your kind of love. Your love is toxic, full of lies and misrepresentations, and no accountability for your actions. I accept responsibility for ignoring things I would normally notice because I loved you wholeheartedly. I put too much trust in a man after learning as a child that men will fail you. The betrayal is too deep. I'm sick of hearing excuses. I don't have the energy to try again. I hope you find whatever you're looking for, but it's never been me. Goodbye; my coffee is getting cold," Sahara firmly states as she retrieves her coffee from the counter and exits the coffee shop.

Jackson slumps in his chair, unable to believe his marriage is over. *Sahara, I'll never give up on us or on you! I'll show you we belong together. I'm not interested in anyone else,* Jackson thinks to himself as he continues to plan how to reclaim his wife.

Sahara finishes her coffee before leaping from her car and sprinting toward Mr. Fuentes' office. She checks her watch. "Shit. Nine forty-one! Jackson, you asshole!" Sahara murmurs as she approaches Mr. Fuentes' receptionist, sweating like a whore in church and out of breath.

"Are you okay, ma'am?" inquires the receptionist.

"Yes, I have a meeting with Mr. Fuentes at ten o'clock. Sahara Patterson-Andrews is my name."

"Mrs. Andrews, I'll notify Mr. Fuentes of your arrival. Please take a seat."

"Thank you very much! Could you please direct me to your restroom?"

"Sure. Go a quarter of the way down the hall to the left."

The conversation with Jackson frazzled Sahara's nerves and tied her stomach in knots. She tries to use the restroom while repeating affirmations to herself, then washes her hands and splashes water on her face. Sahara looks in the mirror, patting her face dry with paper towels, and says aloud, "You can do it! You've got this! You're up to the task! It's my turn!"

She fixes her hair, applies lip gloss, and gives herself a once-over before leaving the bathroom. Mr. Fuentes is standing in the doorway of his office as she walks back to the sitting area.

"You might as well continue walking. Let's go, young lady."

"Good morning, sir. I hope you're having a good day so far."

"I got here without my wife yelling at me before I left, so I did something right today. Let's get down to business, shall we?"

"Sure, okay," Sahara responds.

Sahara will meet with Mr. Fuentes three times per week for the next few weeks. He is impressed by her quick wit and attention to minute details. After three months, Zion, Mr. Fuentes, and Sahara search for a quaint minimalist office space for her new venture Say My Name Marketing.

CHAPTER SIXTEEN

Remember Me

S AHARA AND HER KIDS ARE adjusting well to their new routine, and Zion is relishing having kids back in his house. Their presence has lessened the repressed grief, regret, and guilt he has been carrying around since Champagne's passing.

"It's nice to see you smiling," Sahara says to her father.

"These days, I have a lot to be happy about. My favorite girls have been keeping an old man company, and I have a date with Zena Whitcomb tonight."

"After everything you've been through, you deserve to be happy. I hope everything works out for you, Daddy."

"Let us not put the cart before the horse. It's only dinner," Mother Spencer declares as she enters the kitchen. "Good morning, everyone."

"It's fantastic that Daddy is getting back into the dating scene. He's going out to dinner with Zena tonight."

"I heard all of you. Watch out for that one. She's not like anyone else I've met in the past. I'm going to pray about this for sure."

"Mom-Mom, I thought you'd be glad that Dad isn't working himself to sleep or staying alone in this big house. We won't be here for too much longer. It would be great if he could find love again."

"I'd like Zion to find a good wife, not just a woman. There is a distinction between the two."

"Momma, I'll proceed with caution because you've never led me astray... But take it easy. I'm not gullible. Put some trust in me and my decisions," Zion asserts.

"I apologize if I offended you. It is a mother's instinct to protect her children, regardless of age. I love you and will always want the best for you."

"I understand, Momma." He kisses Mother Spencer on the cheek and says, "I love you more." He says to everyone, "Have a wonderful day, ladies. I'm on my way to the office."

"Bye, Daddy. I love you!"

"Baby girl, come sit with me in the living room," Mother Spencer instructs. Sahara follows and takes a seat on the plush velvet sofa next to her grandmother.

"I need you to listen to me, and listen well," Mother Spencer begins. "For a long time, your sisters' resentment toward you regarding their mother and how she died went unaddressed. Zion never wanted to confront it, but I believe that was a mistake for which you have paid dearly. Our silence encouraged their behaviors. We thought that covering them, ignoring their actions, and praying would solve the problem. His guilt and desire not to speak ill of Champagne caused him to bury many long-overdue conversations." She came to a halt and patted Sahara's hand.

"It matters how you allow people to treat you, but it matters even more how you treat them in return. I pray for my granddaughters daily because their mother instilled such evil in them. She was very convincing and embodied a type of godliness to the point of causing strife among the saints. Champagne had a distinct evil personality that only Zion and I witnessed.

"Dominique was his solace, even if it was wrong. You get what you see with your mother. I've always regarded her as a daughter. Champagne did things for the sake of show, and those kids were her show ponies. Only God can help them see themselves. Corrin loves her mother, God bless her soul. I'm worried because I see her getting closer to this Zena woman." She takes another breath and frowns before looking Sahara in the eyes and firmly continues.

"I know you all look at me as family, not realizing the spiritual mantle God has graced upon my life. I am a divinely empowered woman. He has bestowed upon me the gift of discernment, which allows me to hear people's thoughts at times. I've been living for the Lord and preaching His gospel for nearly fifty years. It was the best decision I'd ever made. I wish I could change or redo some things, but what's done is done. I'm far from perfect, but I have a sinking feeling that something terrible is about to happen to this family.

"When I met Zena, my spirit was at odds with her spirit. She has a dark secret and a plan for my son. There are so many unanswered questions surrounding her. Why is she here after all these years? Champagne never mentioned this woman to any of us, although she knows so much about the family. Whatever happens, I need you to be strong and watch your back! People will say one thing and do something different, so speak less and listen more. Allow people to show you who they are.

"Learn God's perspective on you by reading the Bible and praying more. You're an amazing mother and an extraordinary young woman. If you mess up, accept responsibility, and move on. To have a good heart like yours, you must guard it at all costs. You must keep it from falling into the wrong hands. Keep in mind that your children are watching. It's what you do, not what you say, that they'll follow as an example of. Don't let the opinions of others keep you bound to your past. People in the church sometimes make a bigger mess than those in the world. There are unresolved issues in everyone's past. The primary orators need to be silenced before they let a bone fly out their mouth from one of their skeletons. You've fallen down, but you keep picking yourself back up to shine as an inspiration.

"You're being far too hard on yourself. Stop doing that!" Mother Spencer squeezed Sahara's hand. "You do better when you know better. Allow the past to remain in the past so that you can move on with your life. Fast, pray, and ask God to help you become the woman He sees you as. Some people may have to be cut off. People may become upset if they see you changing for the better, which you are. Never dim your light to make mediocre people feel better about themselves. I'm an old lady now. I've seen and experienced a lot, but God has kept me. He'll keep you as well.

"You have lovely children. Don't allow anyone to be around them or say things contrary to what you teach them. Don't allow your children to go over to their friends' houses if their parents don't like you.

"I won't be here for much longer. I want you to remember me and what I taught you. You must learn to see and not see, to hear and not to hear. Not responding is sometimes a response. Having you as a granddaughter has been one of the most rewarding experiences of my life. Life has thrown some hard punches at you, but you're still standing. You're the comeback kid, my dear child. I'm extremely proud of you. Keep coming back when life hits you hard. After a while, you'll reflect on your life and realize that nobody but God brought you here. Something is going to happen, but God has already told me you will survive it. Believe in Jesus and pay attention to that small voice. It sounds like you, but it's Him leading and guiding you. I'm not sure why I felt compelled to tell you all of this. It was not my intention at all. God is the best judge, and all is well, beloved," Mother Spencer concludes.

Sahara clings to her grandmother as tears stream down her cheeks. "I appreciate you more than you will ever know, Mom-Mom!"

~

"Hello and welcome to Indulge. Have you made a reservation?"

"Yes. Spencer, a table for two."

"Right this way, Mr. Spencer," the host responds as she leads Zion and Zena to their table.

Zion pulls Zena's chair out for her.

"Thank you."

"You're welcome, and I must say you look stunning tonight."

"Thank you once more. I'm not used to a man giving me this much attention. It's been a long time."

"Same here. I'm embarrassed to admit I'm a little nervous and I don't get much attention from men either," Zion admits.

Zena chuckles, then asks, "Is something wrong?" when she notices a cross look on his face.

"No, I'm guessing you and Champagne had a very close relationship. In that moment, your laugh reminded me of her," Zion admits.

"We were more like sisters, but we lost touch when my father moved us out of the country for his job. I apologize for upsetting you," Zena responds.

"I'm not bothered. I haven't allowed myself to talk about Champagne with anyone other than my immediate family in years. I suppose Sahara was correct."

"What do you mean?"

"She told me I need to talk to someone about my past feelings in order to move on."

"She sounds bold to suggest that to a parent."

"Sahara is brave, fearless, and a great help to me. She thinks I saved her, but it was her and those grandchildren who saved me from my mundane existence." He took a breath. "Please accept my apologies. This isn't your average date-night conversation."

"I appreciate your candor and willingness to express your feelings."

"It's been a long time since I've felt able to express myself as freely as I do professionally, personally. You put me at ease."

"That may be the best date-night compliment I've ever received."

"While we're being so open, Zena, may I ask you a question?"

"Sure. Anything."

"This question hurts to ask because of how close you and Champagne were, but I feel I must. I remember nothing about that infamous first night we had sex. On my way home from football practice, I recall her asking me for a ride. In the car, we had an amicable exchange that didn't really go anywhere. She offered me one of her father's lagers as a thank you for the ride home and she took me on a tour of her house. For what it's worth, I drank fewer than half of the beer. The next thing I remember, I'm awake in her bed. Did Champagne ever bring up that night?"

As Zion told his tale, Zena reflected on her past. She recalled giving Zion a bottle of beer containing several of her mother's sleeping pills she had crushed and hidden inside.

"No. After finding out she was expecting Corrin, she told me it was a lovely, memorable evening."

"Forever, I charge that beer. It was as if I had no control over my own life after that. I stayed because Champagne's father was adamant about protecting his daughter's honor and preventing her from being publicly shamed for being a teen mom. Because of the promise I made to my mother was the reason I didn't follow in my father's footsteps and abandon the family. Since my children didn't sign up to be here, they were the reason I kept going. It was a prison trying to maintain the image Champagne was so set on projecting to the world. For the sake of the kids, I stayed even though I was stuck between a rock and a hard place: damned if I do; damned if I don't. Nobody has ever inquired as to the specifics of my life goals. They only informed me and imposed these requirements on me. It took away my voice or choice in the matter. The days blended into one another until I found a place at work to devote myself." He halted to catch his breath.

"Don't misunderstand me," he went on. "My life has been wonderful. My kids are the best! However, remorse is a nasty little bitch! I've often thought about what my life might be like if I'd been able to fulfill the dreams I discussed with Dominique, but I stopped doing so because the thought was too painful.

"And Champagne deserved so much more than I could give her. Despite my best efforts, I could never fall in love with her. When I was younger, I was a coward who should have fought harder for the goals I set for myself. Because the woman I have loved my entire life is half a world away, conquering life with another man. Once upon a time, I thought I was suffering as atonement for having wronged not one but two females."

"So, what do you think now, after all this time has passed," investigates Zena.

"I believe I have settled my debt, and I am now free to pursue whatever opportunities present themselves during the years I still have left."

"This is the second most interesting thing you've said so far tonight."

"You've been my de facto therapist, so I can understand if you're looking for an exit strategy."

"I'm more interested in your development as a person," admits Zion. "I demand that we spend the rest of the night chatting about you. How was it living abroad?"

"The first few years were the hardest by far. Then, I settled there due to a lack of alternatives. It was something I had to grow to appreciate, but I could never forget my home in the United States. With the passing of my parents and husband, I no longer had any ties to the UK and therefore no desire to stay abroad. It was mentioned that Sahara's parents are currently traveling abroad."

"They're over in Africa doing missionary work. It's been over a year since they first arrived. Sahara has two wonderful father figures and a brilliant, supportive mother. Together, we're a formidable force in any arena."

"Absolutely fantastic! Corrin mentioned they were involved in ministry. I did not know they were overseas. It's difficult to serve the Lord in another country, so props to them," Zena replies.

"What are your intentions now that you're back in the states, Zena?"

"If I could, I'd go back and finish some unfinished business from years ago, reconnect with some old friends, and maybe even make some new ones. At the moment, I intend to take in the company around me and relish this tasty meal," Zena responds.

CHAPTER SEVENTEEN

A Ram in the Bush

"**G**OOD MORNING, MOTHER SPENCER, HOW'S your day so far?" asks Sahara.

"My day is always good, especially when I hear from my grandbabies."

"Sorry I haven't been able to organize a girls' night out sooner, but I've been really busy getting my business off the ground. At six-thirty, can we meet at Sototally Delicious?"

"Yes! That sounds like a date. Thank you for thinking of an old woman."

"You ain't old until you're cold. That's what you tell me, right?" Sahara answers playfully.

"So, you listen to me?"

"Yes, ma'am."

"Well, baby girl, I'll see you this evening. Love you."

"Love you more, Mom-Mom."

≈

Sahara rushes to finish the last of her daily chores so she can meet Mother Spencer for dinner on time. Zion is spending his evening taking care of his granddaughters. A local artist gives painting classes on the road. Zion and the kids are having a wonderful night of painting. He has ordered a charcuterie board from Indulge. It has fresh cheeses, meats, vegetables, and fruit on it. They're having so much fun!

Sahara arrives at Sototally Delicious and pulls into the crowded parking lot where she searches for a spot where she can park her car. After a long search, she locates one and drives her car into it. Sahara pauses as she walks away from the vehicle and toward the restaurant. She takes a brief look around, then takes out her phone and sends her father a text to do a quick check on the girls. She is taken aback by the sight of headlights barreling towards her, and then she's grabbed by a tall, dark, and incredibly handsome man. Her cries of distress fill the air as the man embraces her more tightly. He releases his hold and retreats a few steps once safe.

"Miss, are you okay?"

Sahara responds with her hand against her chest, "Yes. Thank you very much!" Despite her distress, she can't help but notice how attractive her hero is. "What is your name? You literally saved my life."

"My name's Blake. Blake Kincaid. Who do I have the pleasure of saving tonight?"

"My name is Sahara Patterson. I'm not sure how I'll ever repay you, so please let me buy you dinner."

"Under one condition."

"Sure, anything. Name it."

"You have dinner with me."

"Well, if you don't mind having dinner with me and my date. My grandmother."

"Grandmothers love me!"

They both laugh as Blake opens the restaurant door and motions for Sahara to enter first. He stays close behind her. The host leads them to a booth where Mother Spencer is expecting Sahara.

"I thought this was a girls' night out. He isn't a stripper, is he? Mine eyes have seen the glory!" jokes Mother Spencer.

Both Sahara and Blake burst out laughing. After Sahara has joined her grandmother on the bench style seating, he sits down across from them.

"This is Blake Kincaid, Mom-Mom. He saved me from becoming roadkill. I was almost hit by a car. I figured the very least I could do was buy him dinner."

"Talk about a ram in the bush! God bless you, young man."

"I'm glad I was in the right place at the right time," Blake says as he looks Sahara in the eyes.

Mother Spencer, sensing the chemistry between the two, says, "I'm going to order takeout. You two should stay and have fun. On my way home, I'm going to stop by Mother Ethel's. Thank you once more, young man; she's precious cargo."

"That is without a doubt," Blake responds as he smiles looking at Sahara. "It's a pleasure to meet you, ma'am. Do you require help with your bags?"

"No. Return to your seat and order something good and expensive." Blake follows Mother Spencer's instructions while fanning her face behind his back, causing Sahara to smile broadly but not laugh.

"I suspect your grandmother is quite the character."

"You have no idea! She's the toughest woman I know, and I idolize her."

They order dinner, laugh, and discuss their favorite sitcoms over a nightcap. The two began the evening as strangers, but their friendship is blossoming.

CHAPTER EIGHTEEN

Block the Blocker

SAHARA HAS BUILT A CLIENT portfolio of top-tier businesses and influencers. Corrin and Jazmine decide to pay Sahara a visit after hearing about her achievements in the marketing industry. The sisters share the address, drive separately, and, to their surprise, arrive at a stunning, modernist structure on an upscale industrial estate.

"Hmm, let's see if the interior is aesthetically pleasing," Corrin says as she and Jazmine make their way to the door. Jazmine covers her mouth with her hand once inside. Corrin blinks quickly and then stares openly.

"Say My Name is pleased to welcome you. Do you have an appointment today with Ms. Patterson?" the receptionist inquires.

"No. Our younger half-sister is not expecting us," Corrin coldly responds, wearing a stony expression. "We wanted to surprise her."

"I will let her know you are here. Take a seat and enjoy our snack bar at your leisure."

Jazmine mutters, "Thank you."

The sound of her high heels striking the white marble tiles alerts Sahara's sisters as they watch her approach.

"Good morning, ladies. Are you lost? What brings you by today? Is Daddy okay?"

"Girl, our father's fine," discloses Jazmine.

Icicles appear to shoot through Corrin's veins as her heart seems to thaw and then pound once more. "We heard about your little business and came to wish you well," she responds.

Jazmine adds, "That's right; it's beautiful here."

Sahara tilts her head to the side and smiles. "I'm so grateful. In less than nine months, my boutique business has made just under one million in profit. I think my little company has done quite well."

"How much of Dad's money is invested in this project," Corrin wonders aloud.

"No more than what he's put into your, Jazmine's, and Dex's businesses. Actually, much less. I've had to learn how to make the most out of the least. I'm a Spencer. I have the same resources as you and have proven to be just as diligent. In my previous job, I developed relationships with clients from various fields." She straightens up and adds, "It's been great seeing you. Thank you both for coming, but I have a meeting in ten minutes. See yourselves out. Have a fantastic day!" Sahara declares as she strides back toward her office.

Corrin stands with her arms crossed in front of her chest, flipping her hair. "Goodbye," she says, through her clenched teeth.

Sahara sits at her desk, trying to soak in the moments she's spent with her sisters. She is overjoyed, thinking about her siblings' reactions to her success.

Corrin and Jazmine exit and are standing outside near their cars talking about what happened between them and Sahara.

"We should give Sahara the benefit of the doubt, Corrin. Our primary concern was that she would take advantage of Dad and use his money. He clearly did not give her as much as he has given us. No matter what happens, she comes back stronger than ever. Whatever this hostility is, I'm done with it! At this point, I'm too preoccupied to care. She will always be Dad's favorite. Nothing we do will ever bring Momma back. I'm tired, and we need to move on."

"What exactly are you saying, Jazz?"

"I'm done with whatever this is or has been. Dad is getting older, and we need to prioritize spending time with him. We've tormented Sahara for years, and she's still here. She's not going anywhere! I care about you, but I'm tapping out. I'm off to the shop. I'll call you later."

Corrin watches Jazmine's car as she drives away. Her nostrils flare as she squares her shoulders in the parking lot near her car.

Jazmine's change of heart enrages Corrin. She slams her car door so hard that the window shatters, sending glass shards flying throughout the vehicle. She grips the steering wheel so tightly her rhinestone encrusted fingernails leave imprints in her hands. As she flees, her tires squeal and smoke, and her thoughts race. She is more determined than ever to seize command of her plan to destroy Sahara.

"How does this little bitch keep winning? I want her to die!" Corrin screams and swerves. Her tears puddle in her eyes and fall like buckets of water. Drivers honk their horns to break her trance and warn her of impending danger.

There is only one person who can truly comprehend what she is going through. Like a fish needs water, Corrin requires her presence in her life. Her guide through the underworld. Her surrogate mother, Auntie Z.

Her receptionist calls on the phone intercom. "Your appointment has arrived, Ms. Patterson."

"Thank you very much. I'll be there shortly," Sahara responds.

As Dex holds up bags from Sototally Delicious, she grins. "CEOs must maintain their strength. You're doing big things in these streets, lil sis." Sahara gives Dexter a side hug and assists him in carrying the bags to her office.

"I assumed you hadn't eaten breakfast and that, like most Spencers, you'd work through lunch. Consider what you achieved when you set your mind to it. You never cease to amaze me." Sahara and Dexter place the bags and food containers on a small conference table in her opulent office.

"Thank you for always being there for me. I don't know what I'd do without you, Dad, and Mother Spencer. I consider myself extremely fortunate to have you all in my life. In terms of surprises, your sisters arrived earlier. They appeared surprised by how well my company is doing."

"I am surprised; you are correct. Perhaps they are passing by to extend an olive branch. It would be the best thing they could do for the entire family."

"I'm not sure what the motivation was, but I'd be willing to have a genuine relationship with my sisters. I'd like for us to get to know each other as you and I have."

"I'll be crossing my fingers. Dad would be overjoyed if that happened. Don't eat all the Souljah rolls while I'm speaking!" Dexter exclaims.

"I can't stop eating them, bro. They are delicious. You said you could tell I was hungry, and I am."

"After you've had your fill, come outside to see the new car I bought."

"All right, baller. I can't wait to see what new toy you got."

CHAPTER NINETEEN

Familiar Spirits

ORRIN HAS BEEN DRIVING AIMLESSLY for nearly an hour and has no recollection of parking in Zena's garage, but that's where she is.

Zena is obsessing over her children, wishing she could spend more time with them as she meticulously cleans her home, making sure everything is in its proper place. When Zena goes outside to empty her trash, she overhears someone crying. She throws the bag in the trash and listens for a familiar voice. Once she sees Corrin's vehicle, she runs toward it, finding tissues and glass covering the passenger seat and Corrin's lap. When Zena taps on her car door, she is fidgeting with the last tissue in a box. Corrin screams and then opens the car door, collapsing into Zena's arms.

"What's bothering you, my child?"

"I despise her! She's robbed me of everything. God help me, I hate her!" Corrin is obsessed with the injustice she has assigned to Sahara simply for being born.

Zena comforts Corrin, who is distressed by her daughter's anguish. "Come on in, kid. Allow me to assist you with this."

"I couldn't think of anywhere else to go, but I knew you'd understand. I really miss my mother. I desperately need her," Corrin says as they walk to Zena's condo.

"I'm here for you right now. Please take a seat." Zena directs Corrin to a leather chaise lounge with a round velvet pillow. Zena drapes a throw across her body as she lies across it. "Rest. I'll prepare a light snack for us."

Zena prepares tea, soft scrambled eggs with cheese, and multigrain toast. She spreads strawberry preserves on the toast before trimming the edges and slicing it diagonally.

"Anytime is a good time for breakfast," Zena says, adding each item to a tray table. She runs her hand across Corrin's forehead.

"How long have I been asleep?"

"Just long enough for me to make us brunch."

Corrin sits up, her back against the chaise arm. Zena places the tray table on her lap, while Corrin scans the food and the room for answers in this strange yet familiar environment.

"What's the problem? Would you like something different?"

"That is not the case. To be honest, I'm a little freaked out by the uncanny similarities between you and my mother. You've made one of my favorite dishes just like Mom used to. You even cut the bread's edges. This place smells exactly like my childhood home. Those apple-cinnamon candles were a favorite of Mom's. You embody twins rather than best friends."

"Your mother and I were extremely close."

"'Close' is an understatement," Corrin says. "More like familiar spirits. It confirms that coming here was the right thing to do for myself. When I'm with you, I feel so much of my mother's spirit. That is a wonderful gift and a blessing to me."

Zena refuses to make eye contact with Corrin. Zena inquires, "Are you able to tell me what caused you to be so upset?"

"Can I tell you the truth without fear of being judged?"

"I have no right to pass judgment on you. I'm here to listen in the same way that your mother would."

"Thank you very much. This whole situation with Dad and this cretinous child has been a thorn in my flesh. I remember Mother loading us into the car and driving us to his office. We'd ride by that whore's house every now and then to see if Dad's car was in her driveway. We saw him kissing that woman while she sat on his desk once in his office. When we drove by her house another time, her curtains were drawn and we could see her and father laughing while drinking wine. The table was scattered with food. He never noticed us. That's how I've always felt, unseen by my father, but there's an undeniable bond between him and Sahara. They even complete one another's sentences.

"Mother would send us back to the car, claiming that it wasn't Dad. That home-wrecking whore duped him. I trusted my mother. Dad loved us and Mom when he was with us. Our lives were idyllic until he found out Sahara was his daughter. I believe his infidelity, combined with the fact that he fathered a child with that woman, pushed Mom over the edge. Jazz and I would overhear their discussions. They never spoke lovingly to each other again after that. Sahara turned our lives from sugar to shit, and I despise her for it!

"Dad forgives her no matter how bad her decisions are when they affect her children. I just want her to leave! Every time I see her, I relive my mother's death and recall my parents' arguments. Her mother's use of her body to entrap and seduce my father is imprinted in my mind. I truly hate her! I despise her! I loathe her! She's taken everything I hold dear—my mother and father—and is now prancing around my childhood home. She must pay for her actions!" Corrin's resentment boils over as she recalls traumatic childhood memories.

"When it was discovered that Zion had fathered a child with Dominique, your mother was not herself. I apologize for the anguish her irrational decisions have caused you all. Champagne adored her children more than anything else. If she were still alive, I'm sure she'd want me to assist you. I'm available for whatever you will need. You have the right to express yourself. Don't let anyone convince you otherwise. According to the Bible, an eye for an eye. A life for a life stolen sounds reasonable to me," Zena says as she brushes Corrin's hair.

CHAPTER TWENTY

Jesus, Fix It!

DEXTER'S BUSINESS IS PROFITABLE, so he spoils himself. Dex arrives at his father's house for their monthly dinner, excited, to find Corrin and Jazmine conversing outside.

"Okay, little bro. I see you stunting on them. This is nice!" exclaims Jazmine.

"I did not know hosting fun nights was so lucrative," snarks Corrin.

"Big sis, that almost sounds patronizing or like shade."

"Has Dad seen this extravagant purchase?"

"No, Corrin."

"What has Dad seen?... Oh, my goodness. It's an orange Bentley Continental GT convertible," Zion, surprised, says.

"Orange Flame, to be exact," Dexter says. "I expected you to be upset. You've expressed a desire for us to spend modestly over the years, but I fell in love with this beauty the moment I saw her."

"Enjoy the rewards of your hard work, son. You earned it. Want to take an old man for a spin?"

"Let's go!"

"We'll be right back, pretty girls. I'm looking forward to being chauffeured for a change."

As they cruise down the highway, father and son talk, listen to music, laughing as they imagine Champagne's reaction to Dexter's vehicle purchase.

On their way back to Zion's, flashing red and blue lights appear, followed by sirens. Dexter considers his speed and slows down to allow the police cruiser to pass, but the cruiser remains in the lane, heeling them. Dexter pulls onto the shoulder.

"Why are they stopping me? Siri, I'm being pulled over," Dexter says into his phone as his father, sisters, and Mother Spencer all receive his location notification.

An officer approaches the driver's side. "Evening. License and registration," the officer snidely requests.

"What did we do to be pulled over?" Zion asks.

"There have been a few car thefts in this area. If you boys don't produce the paperwork for this car, I'll have to report it stolen."

"Boy? I'm old enough to be your father. I demand you call your supervising officer to this scene immediately!"

"It's not an issue, Dad. In the glove compartment I have all of the paperwork for this vehicle." Dexter reaches across his father's lap to open the glovebox, revealing a black flashlight on top of the documents.

"Gun, gun, gun!" the officer yells into his radio, launching a hail of bullets into the vehicle, splattering blood across the cream-colored leather.

"Dexter! Dexter!" Zion screams. "What have you done?" he yells at the cop. "Request an ambulance! Son, son, get up!" Zion takes the flashlight from glove compartment and throws it at the officer. "It's a fucking flashlight!"

The overzealous officer steps back from the car and calls for an ambulance. When Chief Parsons arrives at the scene the officer immediately tries to explain what happened, but the chief pushes him against the cruiser when he notices Zion covered in his son's blood.

"Do you have any idea who that is? That's Zion Spencer, one of the police union's most generous donors and staunch supporters."

As the emergency personnel remove Dexter's terrifyingly lifeless body from the car and place it on a stretcher, Chief Parsons rushes to Zion's side. The blood of his son stains Zion's clothes.

"Mr. Spencer, I will personally find the underlying cause of this senseless tragedy," Chief Parsons says, nervously.

"You better hope my son lives, because God will not be able to save you from my wrath," Zion says as he steps into the ambulance to accompany his son to the hospital.

They rushed Dexter into surgery once he arrives at the hospital. Zion uses FaceTime to contact his immediate family. "During a traffic stop, an officer shot Dex. I'm at the hospital. It doesn't look good, you guys. Could you please bring me a change of clothes? I'm drenched in Dex's blood…" Zion bursts into tears, jolting his family to their core. He's hyperventilating and can't speak clearly.

Sahara is triggered and immediately hangs up the phone. Corrin and Jazmine make arrangements for their significant others to meet them at the hospital.

Mother Spencer's plea is gut-wrenching. "Oh, Jesus! Jesus, fix it, Lord! I am calling, calling, calling, on Jesus! Fix it right now, God. Lord, nothing is too hard for you. You are Adonai. God of total authority! You are El Elyon. God who we trust. You are El Shaddai. God of all power! You are Jehovah-Rapha. Our healer. You are Jehovah Shalom. Prince of Peace. You are Immanuel. God with us. You are Elohim. You are everywhere. Lord, we need you to be a doctor and touch, heal, and save my grandson. Do it, God! Fix it, Jesus! I know you can do it. In Jesus' matchless name, amen. We're all on our way, son."

The call ends as everyone rushes to be with Zion at the hospital. Before heading that way, Jazmine retrieves a tracksuit and sneakers from her dad's closet, as well as a trash bag for his bloody clothes.

Sahara is the first to arrive at the hospital, while Zion's mind races with questions. As he rubs the nape of his neck, his chest tightens.

"Daddy!" Sahara screams and rushes into his arms, clutching him tightly.

"Will I ever be able to protect my children? I can't lose my son. God, why? I can't do this again! It should've been me."

As they enter the waiting area, Corrin, Jazmine, their partners, and Mother Spencer overhear Zion yell those words.

"It should not have been either of you," Mother Spencer declares as she rounds the corner, overcome by the sight of Zion's blood-soaked clothes. Sahara tries to console her, while Corrin and Jazmine cling to their crying father, needing to be close to him.

Jazmine hands him his clean clothes and sneakers in a bag. When Zion entered the men's bathroom, his eyes red and swollen from crying, he removed his shirt and found that Dex's blood had penetrated it and stained his chest. Zion weeps while wiping his son's blood from his chest, then splashes water across his chest to speed up the traumatic cleansing. The white paper towels fade from red to a pale pink, then back to white.

He then takes off his trousers, socks, and shoes and places them in the bag Jazmine gave him. He puts on the tracksuit and sneakers after splashing icy water across his face and neck, then stares at his aging reflection.

"I've never been a praying or Godly man. I've been quite the opposite. I've been selfish and arrogant, an adulterer, and a liar. The only good thing I have in my life is my children. I've messed up so many times, but the love of my children gives me strength to do and be who I am. Please, Father God, in the name of Jesus, I will do anything if you save my son's life. A life for a life. I will give you my life. This is my vow to you, oh, most Holy One. I'm sorry for every sin, indiscretion, error…every bad thought…I am sorry! God, I am sorry," pleads Zion.

"Your son will not die. A life for a life," says the Spirit of the Lord.

Zion collapses to the floor, praising, worshiping, and thanking God.

When Mother Spencer walks to the bathroom to check on Zion, she overhears him praising God. She covers her mouth with her hand. Her son's prayers to God reinvigorate her, and she begins to speak in unknown tongues in the hallway.

Zion and Mother Spencer rejoin their family members in the waiting area for the surgeon. They've been there for several hours.

"Your brother will recover. He'll be fine; I promise," asserts Zion. The sisters do not share their father's optimism and prepare for the worst, even though they hope he is correct.

The surgeon enters the waiting room a few minutes later. "Is this the Spencer family?"

"Yes," Zion confirms.

"Dr. Barkley is my name. Dexter was shot multiple times in the torso, causing damage to his spleen, gallbladder, and one of his kidneys. We were able to save the damaged kidney after a transabdominal exploration. We will leave a drain in his abdomen for a short time. We were successful in removing the bullets and shell fragments. He has multiple visceral lesions, but if he follows protocols and avoids infections, Dexter will recover completely. He'll be monitored in the ICU recovery room for at least seven to ten days, and he'll be given IV antibiotics. We will keep track of his progress at all times. He's a very fortunate young man."

"Thank you for the wonderful news, doctor. God is great!" Zion says as he extends his hand to Dr. Barkley.

The family members hug each other, relieved. They understand Dexter will have a long road to recovery, but they thank God for what He has done.

CHAPTER TWENTY-ONE

Your Enemy, My Friend

DEXTER HAS SPENT SEVERAL MONTHS recuperating at his father's house, with his entire family by his side at all times. Zena pays daily visits, relieving family members who assist with Dexter's care. When Sahara walks in, she is sitting on the love-seat, talking with Dexter, who is lying across the sofa.

"Hey, hey. What's up, big bro? Hello, Ms. Zena."

Instead of speaking to Sahara, Zena gives her a cold, insincere smile and raises her hand to wave.

Dexter notices but keeps his lovely younger sister entertained. "I'm fine, sis. I wish everyone would stop making a big deal about me. I'm eagerly awaiting my return to work."

"Please indulge us. We love you," Sahara explains.

"This could have taken a completely different turn. We could be preparing for a funeral," Zena snaps.

"That sounds like something my mother would say if she were still alive," Dexter says to Zena.

"You sound like Dad when you say you're ready to return to work. Where is he?" Sahara inquires as she surveys the room.

"He went shopping for a few groceries. Dex has been eating anything that hasn't been nailed down."

"Hey, Auntie Z. I'm a healing young man. I don't have anything else to do. Everyone treats me like I'm sickly. I can only take one day at a time so many times. I want to get back to my normal life."

"Bro, put your health first. You have a great team that has stepped up and done a great job of taking care of your business. Nothing has been left behind. It's only been a few months, and you'll be able to go back to work in a few more weeks. I'm sure you don't want to do anything that will set you back, so just take it easy and let us help you as much as we can."

"Your body has been through a lot," says Zena. "From the inside out, it needs to get better. Your dad wants to make sure you need nothing when he isn't here."

"Bro, please don't get mad if we want to hold you a little tighter and a little longer. I remember being shot when I was a kid. Your family will treat you well, so let us do it. I love you, and I'm glad God let you stay with us." Sahara stops to give Dex a peck on the cheek.

"I'm going back to the office because it's clear you're in expert hands. I love you so much." Sahara holds her brother in her arms and kisses the top of his head.

Dexter tells Sahara, "I love you more," as he squeezes her hands. "We'll talk again soon."

"Bye, Ms. Zena."

Zena waves bye to Sahara.

"Auntie Z, can I ask you a question," asks Dexter as Sahara exits. "Sure. Anything."

"Have any of my sisters said anything bad about Sahara to you?"

"Why on earth would you ask me that?"

"You don't seem to like her. I grew up with sisters, so I'm used to reading women well."

"I'm aware of their turbulent relationship, but I make my own decisions about people," Zena says.

"That's great news, because Sahara is the best! Life has thrown a slew of challenges her way, and she has risen like a phoenix. She always triumphs over adversity. I'm older, but I respect her. She has every right to be a witch, but she is kind, warm, and caring. Sahara is even kind to those who are mean to her. She's a lady with class.

"If I may be candid," Dexter continues, lowering his voice a little. "I believe my sisters are jealous of her. Dad loves us all, but their relationship is unique. I don't mind because Dad has always been there for us. I've never questioned his feelings for me, nor have I ever felt betrayed by him. He admired how Mother raised us by upholding the values she instilled in us. As I grew older, I realized Dad loved Mother in his own unique way.

"I loved my mother as well, but she was a strict disciplinarian. She wanted us to be perfect at everything at all times. That is a lot of pressure for a kid. She'd start questioning or arguing with Dad as soon as he walked into the house. He'd frequently walk right back out the door. He cheated, but doesn't the Bible say something about a man who would rather be on a rooftop than in a house with a nagging wife? All I know is that when Mom died, Dad stepped up, and I grew to admire him even more. He'd let us celebrate Mom's birthday and Mother's Day. We'd all say a few words, hoping they'd make it to heaven."

This revelation has overwhelmed Zena. His admiration also enraged her for the bastard who cost her life. She responds, "Those are wonderful memories of your mother. Thank you for sharing them with me. I'm sure your mother hears everything and is overjoyed to see how her children have grown into such accomplished adults. I have an appointment in a few minutes, but I'll check in on you tomorrow. Is that okay?"

"Yes, ma'am."

"I love you, son."

"I love you, too, Auntie."

As Zena is leaving, she runs into Mother Spencer, who is entering the house.

"Good afternoon, dear," Mother Spencer says.

"Is it?" Zena snaps as she walks out the door.

Mother Spencer glares at Zena as she hurries out. "Lord, that woman isn't fit to fool with. Who are you, child, and what do you want with my family?" She watches Zena until she can't see her anymore and then heads into the house, calling, "Where's my favorite grandson?"

"I'm on the sofa, Mom-Mom."

"I saw Zena on the way out. What do you think about her?"

"She seems to care a lot for Dad, Corrin, Jazmine, and me, but I have a feeling she doesn't like Sahara at all."

"I don't think she likes me either, for that matter."

"Really?"

"Yes, sir. You keep your eyes open with that one."

"Yes, ma'am. If someone can't get along with you, then they have a serious problem."

"I can't get rid of the feeling that she's hiding something from us."

"God communicates with you. I'm confident He'll lead you to the truth."

"You are the most intelligent grandson I've ever had."

"I'm the only grandson you have."

"That's why you're so smart. Now let me get in here and see what there is to cook."

"Say less!"

"Say what?"

"Never mind, Grandma."

Zena is still enraged because of Dexter's revelations. Her nostrils are flaring as she rough-handles objects around her house. A thick vein in her neck is filling up with blood as it pulses and pounds like a drumbeat. Zena fantasizes about the violence she wants to inflict on Sahara and laughs menacingly. Sahara is the deep wrinkle in the Spencer family that she must remove in order to appease Champagne!

CHAPTER TWENTY-TWO

The Ditch

THERE'S A STENCH IN THE air, and the room's length is dimly lit. Two beings with wrinkled, hairy faces that resemble hogs with tusks stand as men. They are laughing as they carry out their evil plans. The two visible people's bodies resemble cigarette ash; it's impossible to tell males from females. They are tied to a pole and suspended from the ceiling by their hands and feet with their mouths gagged. The only distinguishing feature of humanity is their eyes. The two hog-men turn them over a burning pit, stretching the pole from which their bodies hang. The two tormentors laugh hysterically as the people scream through their gags after stretching and turning the pole over the fire. Hades is this tortuous waiting place for the unrighteous until Judgment Day.

When the hog-men retracted the pole, the ash-people's groans subsided to whimpers. There is an effort to shed tears, but no fluid escapes their eyes. The utter terror on their faces betrays the fact that their brief respite from torture is about to end. The evils beings roast the people in a rotisserie-style fashion, with the pig-men turning the pole at alternating speeds over the fire. As their tormentors take sickening pleasure in their suffering, the two ash-people try to make themselves heard by anyone who might help them break free through their gags. They won't get help or be heard. They have condemned themselves to an eternity of suffering without grace or mercy.

"Detour and repent!"

~

Corrin wakes up sweating and panting from her nightmare. She glances at the time. The time is 5:45 a.m. She then looks over at her husband who is fast asleep. Corrin clears her mind by taking a cold shower. She can't help but think of her mother but thoughts of Sahara interrupt her showering.

"You keep popping into my head, damn it. I have no choice but to get rid of you," Corrin mutters to herself, and her mind goes to Auntie Zena. She laughs to herself as she thinks back on the conversations that the two of them have shared. It is 6:30 a.m. when she emerges from the shower and begins getting ready for the day.

Corrin sends a text to Zena that reads, "I realize you may be asleep, but I'd like to see you today."

"Come by at eight. Is that too early for you?"

"No, ma'am."

Zena sends a text that reads, "Then I'll see you then."

Zena has been giving some serious thought to telling Corrin the truth about her situation. She is sick and tired of the lies, and she wants to take responsibility for her role as the mother of her children. She will need to deliver this mind-blowing revelation to her children with great care if she does not want to cause them any psychological harm.

When Zena's favorite girl, Corrin, shows up at eight in the morning, she takes precautions to ensure that she is well-equipped to make a delicious breakfast for her. Zena has prepared a sumptuous breakfast featuring Belgian waffles, bacon, fruit, cheesy eggs, and orange juice.

"You didn't have to go through all this trouble for me, Auntie."

"I certainly did. How else would you understand how special you are to me?"

"I'm feeling overwhelmed by all of this attention."

"You deserve it," Zena says. "How is Dexter progressing?"

"He's great. This week was his first week back to work."

"Did he say how he's doing?" Zena inquires.

"When I asked Dex, he said good."

"That's terrific news. Thank you, Lord! Corrin, I must confess that some aspects of my past are upsetting to discuss. I've tried to block these thoughts from my mind. Every day, I think about you, your siblings, and Zion."

"Auntie, you've been a blessing to all of us. Whatever the case may be, I'm here to help."

"Awe, that is so sweet," admits Zena.

"When I was younger, I loved my husband and children more than life itself. I made some terrible decisions, and I almost died as a result of them. I have abandoned my family and friends. My father flew me halfway around the world for various experimental treatments. The actual work began when I awoke from my coma. It was difficult to relearn how to walk and care for myself. I was in that coma for years, but I fought hard to recover. My appearance and mobility have changed, so I underwent plastic surgery to feel more at ease in my new body. But my family and my life were never far from my thoughts. I've been gone for so long that I've acquired a British accent."

Zena pauses and takes a breath. "I want to be open and honest with you about my past."

141

"Auntie, you've come through a terrible illness unscathed. When you return home, I'm sure your children and family will greet you with open arms."

"I'm not convinced, so I haven't told them yet."

"Auntie, I'll accompany you to show my support. Are you scared?"

"Yes. I am terrified. I'm not sure it'll be the joyful reunion you're hoping for."

"This will have to happen!"

"Really?"

"Yes. Do you have their phone numbers? I can contact them on your behalf."

Zena scribbles a phone number on paper and hands it to Corrin.

"302-645-17—" Corrin starts reading it aloud, then looks up at Zena, wide-eyed. "This is my contact information. What kind of a joke is this? What is your name?"

"You've known the whole time, my dear child. It's me. Champagne. I am your mother."

"No. You're not telling the truth! My mother is no longer alive! Why would you say something so cruel?"

"Corinthian Spencer! I devoted my firstborn to God's Word. The only child I've ever known who wanted to change the world with a Bible. Don't be afraid. It's truly me. I'm not here to harm you.

"Yes, my lovely, talented, and amazing daughter." The two hold each other tightly as they weep.

They sit, attempting to regain their composure.

"Why did you take so long to tell me? You've been here nearly a year."

"Corrin, I had to double-check…I honestly didn't know whether or not I was going to stay. I couldn't leave after seeing what your lives had been like with Sahara."

"All I can do is deal with the thorn in my flesh."

"There is always something we can do," Champagne says. "We've both had the same desire to get rid of Sahara for years. I have a plan."

≈

Corrin has returned home, her husband Carlito is away on business, and she prepares a lavish surprise dinner for her sister, Sahara.

"Hello?"

"Hello, Sahara. Because of your successful business and the fact that we're sisters, I'd like to talk about how we can continue to grow as a family. I sincerely apologize for allowing my rage to cloud my judgment toward you over the years. Can you come over for dinner tonight? I'd love to make this formal apology in person to clear the air. What do you think?"

Sahara can't think of anything to say. She takes the phone from her ear and looks at it before responding, "Okay, what time?"

"Does seven work for you?"

"Sure. It's perfect," Sahara says.

"Excellent. I'll see you soon."

Sahara suspects a practical joke but hopes her sister is sincere. They have denied her a sisterly relationship for years and she would love for this to be a dream come true and a new beginning for the Spencer sisters.

≈

"Hello?"

"Hi, Mom-Mom."

"Good evening, baby. How are you?" asks Mother Spencer.

"In complete shock!"

"What's the matter?"

"Nothing, I suppose. Corrin invited me to dinner tonight at her house."

"Corrin who?"

Sahara chuckles a little, knowing Mom-Mom is joking. "My sister, Corrin."

"Hmm. I'm curious what that's all about."

"She says she wants to formally apologize to me and that we'll talk about some other things. I hope she's not pranking around on me."

"You've always wanted to be close to your sisters. I know that. I hope it's true for the sake of this family."

"Me, too, Mom-Mom. Love you!"

"I love you even more."

"I'll call you tomorrow to see how it went."

"That sounds good," Mother Spencer says.

"Bye."

"Good night, Sahara."

≈

Sahara completes her tasks at the office and heads straight from work to Corrin's, arriving at seven o'clock. Corrin greets her sister with a hug and a kiss on the cheek as she opens the door with a warm, welcoming smile. Her sister's joy takes aback Sahara, but she hopes this is a change of heart.

"Come in, come in. I'm glad you could attend on such short notice. I made enough for you to take a plate home. Here's a glass of wine. I'll pour myself some as well."

"Thank you for inviting me over, Corrin, but can we get to the point? I'm hoping we can have a relationship as sisters, but what has caused you to change your mind so drastically?"

"You're correct. I'll say it. I've been a bitch to you for years. Since we were children. The way you're handling your business and recovering from your train-wreck marriage proved to me you have Spencer drive. That's something I admire. Plus, Father isn't getting any younger, and we all know how much he wants us to bury the hatchet. It'll take me time but I'm willing, and I'll try to work on treating you more like a sister than an interloper. All I ask is that you be patient with me."

Sahara sips the rest of her wine. Corrin rises and pours another glass for her sister.

"I love you, Corrin," Sahara confesses, letting down her guard. "Regardless of how you treated me. You're an incredible person, and I admire how you command a room. I'd often listen to you speak and cheer inside, thinking, that's my sister. I've prayed many nights for this day to arrive."

As the room spins uncontrollably, Sahara places her hand on her head. "What have you done, Corrin?"

"Whatever do you mean, dear sister?" Corrin replies wickedly.

Sahara's eyes well up with tears as she looks at her sister. She tries to stand but collapses unconscious on the floor. Zena emerges from the kitchen.

"I think I'd have screamed if I had to hear one more whining word," Zena says. "Let's tie her up and put her in the car trunk."

Corrin follows her mother's instructions, and the women drive until they reach a dirt road that leads deep into the woods. Zena parks her car near a casket-length hole she dug earlier.

Within the darkness of Zena's rental car's trunk, Sahara is awakening. Her hands and feet are tied, and they gagged her mouth. Sahara searches for an object with which she can be freed or protected. She removes the padding from the taillights, feels for the wires, and starts to pull on them. She refuses to give up and continues searching for an object to free herself with.

≈

Blake's home is a small cabin situated in the woods. The smooth jazz on the record player, the crackling fire in his wood stove, and the company of his bull mastiff, Butch, have him relaxing the evening away as he sips an ice-cold, frothy beer, thinking about Sahara Patterson and longing to see her. When he notices flickering lights in the distance, he is reclining in his favorite chair near a window. He grabs his automatic rifle, and Butch prepares to accompany him to investigate the source of the flashing lights.

≈

Zena and Corrin exit the vehicle. They gleefully discuss how they will get rid of Sahara while standing beside the trunk. Hearing their conversation, Sahara mulls over how to best position her body to fight once the trunk opens.

"We're in the woods, you idiot! Out here, no one can see or hear you. Stop fucking around with the lights!" taunts Zena loudly.

Sahara recognizes her voice but is perplexed why Zena despises her and would assist Corrin. Sahara begins to kick as the trunk opens. Corrin and Zena sneer at Sahara's attempt to defend herself.

"Have you ever seen anything so pitiful?" Corrin inquires.

"Yes. Her whore of a mother."

Sahara stares at them both, confused, and still under the influence of the drugs they gave her.

"She seems to have something to say," Corrin says as she rips the duct tape and rag from Sahara's mouth. "Speak up, girl!"

"What's the matter with you?" Sahara screams. "You're my sister! I have children! Why are you doing this to our family?"

"Do you hear what she's saying, Mom? Our family. Never was it your family!" Corrin screams. "You take until there is nothing left. You almost took my mother away from me, but she returned to us. She'll make sure Dad and the rest of the family forget about you. Your kids will be better off without you!"

"You're not thinking, Corrin. I forgive you. Let's go home, please! We can discuss this at home. I'm not sure what this woman told you, but your mother is no longer alive! Hurting me will not bring her back."

"Wrong, wrong, and wrong again!" Zena lifts her shirt to show Sahara her bullet-wound scars.

"Champagne!" Sahara exclaims.

"I'm going to finish what I started years ago in the flesh."

Corrin and Champagne drag Sahara out of the trunk while she screams for help near the makeshift grave.

≈

"What the hell have we gotten ourselves into, boy?" Blake asks, rubbing the top of Butch's head. He shines his flashlight on the ladies and recognizes one of them. "Sahara?"

"My name is Sahara!" she says while gasping for air, unable to see who it is because the flashlight beam is so bright.

"I do not know what you ladies have planned here, but I suggest that you be on your way, and please leave Ms. Sahara here with me."

Champagne exclaims, "No more interference!" as she pulls out a small handgun that had been concealed at her waist.

Butch starts charging Champagne, she and Corrin let go of Sahara, and she rolls away from the makeshift grave and towards the car's direction. Champagne run to Butch. She raises her weapon to her shoulder and aims it at Butch, while Corrin follows closely behind her.

Champagne and Corrin are hit by Blake's fire, which is repeated several times. Both of them plummet into the grave that had been prepared for Sahara, shattering their bones in the process. Corrin lands awkwardly on top of Champagne, causing Champagne's rib to puncture her lungs.

Corrin mutters, "I'm sorry, Momma," while her breaths become increasingly shallow and labored.

Champagne, who is choking and gurgling as she drowns in her own blood, asks, "For what?"

"Wasn't able to complete..."

"We'll be together in paradise. I love you."

"I love you, too, Momma."

Corrin feels the gentle touch of Champagne's hand on her back for the last time. As the two women take their final breaths, Corrin gives her mother a peck on the cheek before they both pass away in each other's arms.

Butch is positioned next to Sahara as Blake makes his way toward both of them. He reaches into the pocket of his jeans, pulls out a pocketknife, and frees Sahara's hands and feet. She sits herself up, hugs Blake, and then sobs uncontrollably. Blake transports her on his back until she regains sufficient strength to finish the journey on foot to his cabin. He makes room for her to sit close to the fire and covers her with a blanket.

He then hands her his mobile phone and instructs her, "Call your family."

She dials a number. "Hello there," says Mother Spencer. "I wasn't expecting to hear from you so soon."

"There was a fatal accident. I'm going to send you the address where I am. Is it possible for you to give it to Daddy and ask him to call an ambulance?"

"My dear God. What's happened, child?"

"My sister dug a ditch for me, but she ended up getting hurt when she fell into it. Send any help you can, and I'll explain everything once I've processed this." After hanging up the call, Sahara texted Mother Spencer her current location before handing Blake his phone.

He asks, "Is there anything I can do for you until your family arrives?"

"Yeah. Hold me," Sahara responds softly, burying her head in Blake's chest as she sobs, releasing years of emotional trauma with each tear that falls.

ACKNOWLEDGMENTS

Thank you once again to my favorite editor, Sharon Honeycutt, to Adrijus Guscia for this fire-book cover design, and to Jodi McPhee for the interior design. I would like to thank my family for their support. Most of all, I would like to thank my Chaos Fans for their support and patience and for placing me on the best sellers list! I thank God for this gift of writing He has given me to share the gospel.

ABOUT THE AUTHOR

 **Yolanda Soto** is a Delaware native with extensive experience in education, finance, and management. During her adolescence, she discovered her talent for storytelling, and her favorite English teacher, Ms. Andrews, encouraged her to use her overactive imagination. Yolanda creates a wide range of curriculums for financial literacy and literary programs. She has overcome numerous challenges and uses her life experiences to inspire her audience. Yolanda has three lovely daughters: A' Lonna, Tatyana, and Nylah.